Midnight Sisters

SARAH E. BOUCHER

MW01172972

© 2016 Sarah E. Boucher

All rights reserved.

No part of this book may be reproduced in any form whatsoever, whether by graphic, visual, electronic, film, microfilm, tape recording, or any other means, without prior written permission of the publisher, except in the case of brief passages embedded in printed reviews and articles.

This is a work of fiction. The characters, names, incidents, places, and dialogue are products of the author's imagination. Any resemblance to actual persons, living or dead, business establishments, events, or locales is entirely coincidental.

ISBN 13: 978-1541204164

First Edition: 2016

Cover design by Cindy Iverson
Cover design © 2016 Cindy Iverson

To the besties, sisters-in-law, cute nieces,
sister cousins, and writing queens.
This one's for you, girls.

Jonas

"Jonas." The manicured grounds and the fifty servants faded into the background as Higgins fixed his eagle eye on me.

Automatically, I inspected my groundskeeper's apron. Spotless and hanging in place, for once. My shirtsleeves were rolled to the elbows, and the brown trousers had been laundered yesterday. How could he criticize anything?

Higgins brushed his steel gray hair off his brow, adjusted the collar of his shirt and cleared his throat.

Oh. When your upbringing included more cattle than people, it meant you occasionally forgot to answer when you were addressed. I still preferred the cattle. They were rarely so demanding. "Yes, sir?"

"The ruins," Higgins said. "On your own."

Relief settled over me as I scanned the broad, green grounds and looked past the big house to the ruins tucked behind it. After two months of trailing after Higgins and bearing his scrutiny at every move, it would be my first solo assignment. Excitement welled up inside at the prospect of escaping his watchful eye. For the first time, something besides my farm home, family, and the loneliness associated with them filled me.

"Gather your tools," he waved a hand in the direction of the low stone building where they were stored, "and be off."

I could hardly believe my good fortune. I would be working alone. And I had been sent off without a recitation of The Rule. No matter how I tried to hold it in, a grin pulled up a corner of my mouth. At least I didn't click my heels and break into a jig. That would have really given Higgins something to criticize.

"Jonas—"

His tone put a damper on my glee. *Please, no,* I pleaded inwardly, the grin sliding off my face.

"You know the cardinal rule."

I wanted to roll my eyes. I kept my expression bland. Eighteen was young, but I was old enough to not behave stupidly. Showing impatience had consequences for an undergardener.

"Do not meddle with the Master's daughters."

I had heard the words so many times my ears felt like they would start bleeding. If Higgins knew how pointless it was to fire them at me time and again, he'd save his breath.

"Understood?" Higgins asked with one eyebrow

cocked.

The thought of running back to my family became more appealing with every upward slant of that eyebrow. "Yes, sir."

"Then, off you go."

Not one to press my luck, I ducked into the stone shed. The scent of the dirt floor mixed with mildew enveloped me. I dumped a load of gardening tools into a wheelbarrow and steered it out the door. The *scree* of the wheelbarrow sounded all along the stone path that skirted the manor.

My last position had been at a large country house. It didn't compare to this brick edifice with separate wings for servants and family. The manor loomed over me, like Higgins, my new Master the Earl of Bromhurst, and everything else I encountered lately. The grounds—an expanse of trimmed lawn and flowering beds, a variety of shaped shrubberies, and a cobbled path—stretched between the big house and the forest and were tended by an army of gardeners.

I turned toward the ruins. Situated at a distance from the main house and hemmed in by vegetation, the ruins were more humble than any other spot within the grounds. I looked forward to spending the day weeding the area and trimming bushes and trees back into respectability. I blocked out the sights and sounds of the too-large world and entered the cool ring of trees with a rush of confidence. I felt it dribble away, replaced with a fresh set of worries wriggling in my stomach at the sight of a young woman seated on the crumbled wall.

The mandate to stay away from the ladies of the house rang in my head like an alarm.

The wheelbarrow dropped to the broken paving stones with a clatter, spilling the tools and alerting the girl to my presence. With her knees tucked up under a long gown and her light brown hair spilling over her shoulders, she looked up from her book with a polite smile.

An image of Higgins wielding a hatchet filled my mind. The storm brewing on his face said he wouldn't believe I'd happened upon the girl by chance.

"Don't let me keep you from your work." She closed her book, unfolded her long legs, and stood before me.

I knelt to gather my tools, my thoughts bumbling over one another in their haste to escape the scene.

"You're new, aren't you? What's your name?"

My thoughts froze, like a deer in the hunter's sights. *What was my name?* "Uh, Jonas . . . Selkirk." *Bow*, I heard Higgins growl as clearly as if he were standing beside me, hatchet in hand. *And address her properly, numbskull.* I stood and executed an awkward bow. "My Lady."

"A pleasure to meet you, Jonas," she said, her oval face open and friendly. "I'm Lady Ariela Spencer." She didn't add that she was the Master's eldest daughter. I knew that already.

I glanced away, charmed and confused by the young woman before me. To my knowledge, Lord Bromhurst's daughters never spoke to anyone beyond the inner household staff. The servants whispered that the ladies did so because they saw themselves as superior to the rest of us. As I watched Ariela, the sunlight gilding her hair, her eyes bright and welcoming, I questioned everything I'd been told about her.

"You know," Lady Ariela remarked, "you have a listening face, Jonas."

I wasn't sure how to respond. If my brothers had said such a thing, I'd have tossed them into a nearby cowpat. Higgins' stern expression came to mind again, the blade of his hatchet catching the light. I reverted to my training, fished a trowel out of the wheelbarrow, and knelt to clear the area of weeds.

"My sister Brisella is like that," she continued. "She's the perfect confidante. She fixes those doe eyes of hers on me and I find myself spilling all kinds of secrets."

Jealousy pierced me at her words. *Why should I care that she confides in her sister?* I asked myself, scraping away at the ground for a moment, the rasp of the trowel against stone unbelievably loud.

"What about your family?" she asked.

I could have laid out my entire life story in less than two minutes. But farm boys were more used to the comings and goings of barnyard animals. Before a young woman like Lady Ariela, my tongue twisted and my thoughts tangled.

I pushed the words out. "We have a farm in Dennisford."

"That's quite a distance," she said, toying with the pages of her book. "Several weeks' journey, at least. Near Stone, isn't it?"

I nodded.

"So far away from your family. Don't you miss your mother?" The inquiry was arrow straight—not *Don't you miss your family?* but *Don't you miss your mother?*

"Yes." I couldn't find words to describe the woman who was always a-bustle, quick to command, reprimand, and comfort. The familiar loneliness settled beside the worries wrangling in my chest.

"Me too."

Sorrow reflected in her eyes, so much deeper than mine. Lady Ariela had probably only been fourteen when her mother had died and she became both mistress of the house and mother to her younger siblings. The urge to bury her in an embrace and ease her sorrow seized me. I looked down at my hands, hardened by labor and unfit for the task of giving comfort. I tightened my grip on the trowel, feeling more uneasy by the second.

"I'm sorry," she said softly, "I've made you uncomfortable. Forgive me, Jonas." After a moment, she asked, "Do you like working here?"

I shrugged and kept my eyes on the ground.

"It used to be such a peaceful place . . ."

Sneaking a glance at her, I noted the dreaminess softening the curves of her face, banishing all but a hint of sadness.

"When Mama was here, we were happier. Her presence made Father more tolerant, and my sisters sweeter." The corners of her mouth turned down. "That's all changed now."

I scraped away, neither discouraging her from continuing nor joining in the conversation. I'd never felt more out of place. At the same time, I'd stay until she sent me away.

"And what do you think of the parade of noblemen?" she asked next. Did girls' minds always flit from subject to subject like this? I had no clue what she meant. My face must have said as much.

"I'm sorry. Family joke," she said, with a tiny grin. "Since I turned fifteen, my father has been parading men through here, young and old alike. As long as they're titled." A wry smile lit her face. I wondered if all young women had this many smiles. "Thankfully, my younger sisters are expert at dissuading suitors from wooing."

I raised my eyebrows in question.

"Any time one of the gentlemen shows genuine interest in my sister Brisella or me, our sisters can be relied upon to cause a ruckus."

I had seen the sisters about the grounds. They ranged in age from toddler to teen and were capable of anything from pitching fits to pitching toys, books, knitting needles, and anything else that wasn't bolted down. One footman had almost lost an eye that way.

"In an effort to save the elder sisters from what they termed 'the madhouse,' some noblemen promised to take us far away," Ariela explained. "Early on, we let it be known that any husband of ours would either have to live here or take our sisters along with us."

I couldn't help chuckling.

"It's not funny, Jonas," she protested, though her eyes glowed with mirth. "Have you heard about Larela?"

Lady Larela. I didn't want to admit that I had, but the two-year-old's tantrums were legendary.

"She's a perfect cherub." Sarcasm twisted at her lips. "With the Devil's own temper, of course. Her talent for causing a scene is only outdone by the triplets. They left the womb bickering, I believe."

I snickered, thinking of the three pint-sized girls who never seemed to get along.

"It's extremely effective at driving the men away," Ariela said, putting voice to my thoughts, "but it means lectures from Father and a 'tightening of the reins' as he puts it. Although, as soon as he's done lecturing, we close ranks and develop new schemes."

I watched her as she spoke. I was taken with the way her words were underscored by the play of emotions across her face. Likely that's what caused me to blurt out, "If they allowed themselves to be run off, none of those men were good enough for you anyway, My Lady."

Her eyes flicked to mine, probably surprised that I could form a complete sentence. A new smile, slow as the sun dipping over the hills, curled the corners of her mouth and eyes. My insides turned to jelly and I wondered how I could tease forth that smile in the future.

As if the opportunity would ever arise again. I wanted to hit myself in the head with a shovel for even considering it.

"That's kind of you to say, Jonas," she said, dropping her gaze and running a finger along the spine of the book in her hands. "I never cared for any of them, so it's of little consequence."

Another moment passed. "And you needn't bother with formalities, Jonas. My friends call me Ari."

She deserved better. She deserved titles, mansions, and households of her own. She deserved all the *my ladies* I could muster. More than that, she deserved someone who cherished her. Unspoken assurances of such hung at the back of my throat, cutting off my air supply.

A feminine voice called her name and saved me from further distress. Lady Ariela scrambled to her feet. "Coming, Bree!" she hollered back. "Thank you for speaking with me, Jonas," she said as she shook the creases out of her skirt. Hurrying off, she tossed over her shoulder, "I hope we can meet again soon."

I watched her leave, feeling the excitement of the day drain away like a room darkening when the lights have been extinguished. That one brief conversation had been the brightest spot in all my time at the manor. My family, home, and the lonesomeness that had weighed me down since my arrival faded beside that brief encounter with Lady Ariela Spencer.

Maybe I could make a home here after all.

Maybe I could make a home here after all.

Ariela

I scratched at the day's growth of beard I hadn't had time to shave and attacked a gnarled root with my shovel. The root was a puny thing, but twisted into the soil as it was, it cost me an extra five minutes. This had been so much easier in my early twenties.

I paused to wipe the sweat from my brow, leaned on the handle of my spade, and looked around at the other servants. Most of the men bent over their tasks, industrious as always. The only exception was the nearby fellow with the wide-eyed expression of a trout. Muttering, he prodded at the ground with a backwards hoe.

I rolled my eyes. I'd lost track of the number of times I'd lectured Loomis on the proper use of gardening tools. With him, once was never enough. In fact, a dozen times weren't enough. I asked myself, not for the first time, why it befell me to look after him.

Gregor probably had it in for me.

A hush fell over the men; even Loomis' mumbled curses fell silent. I guessed the cause and looked up. My chest tightened and my breath caught in my throat the way it always did.

They poured out of the main building, as colorful as the blooms nodding over the lawns, and made their way down the stone walkways between the flowerbeds. Their voices and gentle laughter were musical; their footsteps were light.

Great heavens, was I actually waxing *poetic?*

At least the ladies didn't get caught up in the moment. Every one of the twelve—from the youngest in her early teens to the eldest in her late twenties—kept her eyes averted from the workers. They were adept at this, as we too should have been.

A dozen years of training and I still couldn't resist looking up. Amidst so many beautiful women, Lady Ariela should have been difficult to pick out. I located her in the first second. Arm-in-arm with Lady Brisella, their heads were bent together as if sharing secrets. The familiar pang of envy hit me. I listened for her voice, low and amber-hued, rich and captivating. I wished that I could hear her words.

The handle of a rake smashed into my ribs and I bit back a cry, treating the individual beside me to a venomous look. Gregor, holding the rake in question and not looking at all remorseful, hissed out, "Jonas Selkirk, close your mouth and get back to work."

I rubbed at my sore ribs and scowled at Gregor before resuming my labors. He might have given me a

12

new bruise, but he was right. What I was doing was unwise. I prodded at the ground in my best imitation of Loomis, then glanced up. The object of my affections drew even with me. Her scent, more potent than roses at midday, reached me even though she was still a few paces away.

Lady Ariela Spencer. The syllables rattled around my skull like the most powerful of magic spells, knocking loose any rational thoughts. No matter how many times I saw her, my knees went wobbly. At the same time I felt like I possessed the strength of a score of men.

Stupid, stupid Jonas.

The pair of sisters strolled past, Lady Ariela's arm tucked through her sister's.

"Ari," Lady Brisella said, "Where shall we go today?"

I listened, ready to catch any word. Ari tipped her head to the side—did she know how fetching that was?—and seemed to consider the question well before answering. "The pond, don't you think, Bree? It should be empty this time of day. Perfect for a private chat."

"For half an hour, at least."

I blew out a breath and watched them stroll down the path that curved toward the pond.

"What's wrong with you?" Gregor growled, once again poking at me with the rake, though this time less vehemently. "You know where harboring such feelings will lead, Jonas. Do you want to lose your position?"

I glared, first at the offensive gardening implement,

then at him. "Of course not."

"Then do your work," he barked, returning my glare. "The men look up to you."

I liked Gregor. True, he had become rather puffed up after being named Head Gardener—an understandable promotion given the years of hard work he'd put in—but he had wasted no time in raising me to my current position as one of his assistants. He deserved to know the truth.

Except in this instance. "You're right," I lied. "I'll be more careful."

"Good." Satisfied, he turned his attention back to his work. "There's a special place in Hell reserved for servants who forget their station, Jonas."

Like I'd never heard that before. It had been a favorite recitation of Higgins, Gregor's predecessor. Even so, it rankled like a burr caught in my stocking, chafing at every step.

I waited, bending all my attention to finding the rest of the roots and yanking them from the ground. All about me, tools scraped, words passed between friends, and more curses passed Loomis' lips. The minutes ticked away. Finally, Gregor's groan met my ear.

"What's wrong with you man?" Gregor growled. "Can't you tell the difference between a flowering shrub and a weed?"

Loomis shrugged. Clearly he could not. He had spent fifteen long minutes uprooting a shrubbery that Gregor had planted years ago. Loomis' indifference only increased Gregor's annoyance. His tirade would not be short-lived. I leaned my shovel against a nearby tree trunk and slunk away.

Gregor's voice rang out behind me. "How long have you been at this, Loomis? Five years? Six? Surely you should have learned something of use by now!"

Loomis grumbled, the sound muffled as the distance stretched between us.

"What do you mean Jonas told you which plants to pull out?"

I clapped a hand over my mouth while I ducked around the corner of the manor. There wasn't time for laughter. There were less than fifteen minutes left.

සංඥ

"Where can he be?" Ari asked no one in particular as she threw pebbles into the pond. She sat on the bank, her legs curled up under her full skirt. Her straight nut-brown hair parted over her brow and framed her slim face. Her lips tucked into a frown.

"Lady Ariela, are you talking to yourself again? What would your father say?"

She hopped up at the sound of my voice. Ignoring my teasing, she turned with a smile and reached out to take my hands. "What took you so long? Didn't you understand my message?"

I chastised myself for wanting to take her in my arms, and made myself hold her fingertips lightly. "It was Gregor again. He's ruthless with a rake handle."

"Oh, my poor Jonas." Her tone was more mocking than sympathetic, but I thrilled to the possessive *my*. As with most of our encounters, it was both exhilarating and irritating.

"Come sit by the lake," Ari continued, "and we'll have our talk." She motioned for me to sit beside her on the bank. I longed to sling an arm around her shoulders. I made myself sit at least six inches away and fold my arms tightly over my chest.

"So," she said with a twinkle in her eyes. "We have a plan."

This came as no surprise—something was always brewing in that clever mind of hers. Usually trouble.

"When don't you have a plan, Ari?"

"All right, have it your way." Her lips pulled into a pout. "When I'm not making plans, I'm planning to make plans. Satisfied, Jonas?"

I unfolded my arms and leaned back to more fully take in the flash of annoyance in her eyes. I'd never met a woman more beautiful or intelligent, and considering her family, that was saying something. A grin crept over my face.

"If you don't want to hear what it is, why don't you go back to work?" She lifted her chin and made shooing motions with one hand, like a queen dismissing an underling. "I'm sure Gregor has noted your absence by now."

Of its own accord, one of my hands reached for hers, closing over the slim fingers before I could draw it back. I cleared my throat, hoping my action would only add sincerity to my declaration. "I'd love to hear about your latest plan, Lady Ariela."

Her cheeks pinked as she dropped her lashes, her lips curving into the smallest of smiles. My heart stopped for a second before she lifted her eyes once again and sailed into a recount of her latest scheme. "Father's being a perfect barbarian. It's always: 'Young ladies should do this' and 'Young ladies should do that.' If it was horse riding or observing plants or animals in their natural habitats, I'd have no objection. However, they're always the most tedious things. Needlepoint, lessons in Latin, and other such nonsense."

I watched the play of irritation across her face. I enjoyed it even more when it wasn't aimed at me. "Don't forget the lessons on deportment," I added.

"Exactly! It's enough to drive a woman mad."

"So?"

"We've found a way around him."

I raised my eyebrows.

"I know what you're going to say. We always try to get around him and it never works. However, this time we've considered every scenario." That type of talk, revealing the workings of a bright mind, made her intellect as attractive as her pretty face.

"Something always happens," I reminded her. "Like the time Lady Larela tied all the embroidery thread into knots to get out of finishing her sampler?"

"She didn't have to do needlework for a month, but only because Father made her untangle every last strand. That's Lari." She tipped her gaze skyward in a silent plea for patience with her youngest sister. "She's

17

far too impetuous to think things through."

"How will you avoid that particular pitfall?"

Her lips curved into her widest grin, the mischief-filled one that raised my pulse more than I cared to admit. I hoped she couldn't feel it thrumming in my fingertips. "You'll know when it happens," she said airily, drawing her fingers from mine and tilting her chin to look down her nose at me, even though I was a good head taller.

My hand curled into a fist. "Then why did you ask me here, Ari?"

Her eyes flicked to mine at the curt tone. "If you hadn't made me wait a quarter of an hour, I'd have revealed the whole thing at once, Jonas Selkirk."

I shook my head and kept the growl from rumbling up my throat. Befriending a clever woman was a frustrating undertaking. Almost as frustrating as being in love with one. I eyed the pond, thinking I could douse my exasperation by leaping in.

Ari leaned close enough to whisper in my ear, "I'm glad we're friends, Jonas." Her breath tickled my neck and her flowery perfume chased away all trace of irritation. I could do no more than breathe her in.

She stood. "I must go. Bree will be waiting." She treated me to the impish grin again. "I promise to tell you everything soon. Trust me, Jonas, this plan is foolproof."

Wordlessly, I watched her leave, noting the graceful glide of her steps. As she reached the line of trees circling the pond, she smiled back at me before she disappeared from view. With the parting image fresh in my mind and the prospect of another meeting, the pond no longer looked inviting. Its fetid waters would do little to improve the situation, as Loomis had proven time and again when he'd been dragged from its wet embrace.

ଈଔ

I waited a full five minutes so we wouldn't be seen leaving together, then I strode out of the cover of the trees. With my head in the clouds and my heart replaying Ari's last words, the hand closing around my upper arm caught me off-guard.

"I know what you've been doing."

My heart pounding, I spun around.

"Braden?" The name tumbled off my tongue. He was the last person I'd expected to see.

The redheaded undergardener glared back at me, his green eyes flashing. Beneath the white shirt and brown apron, his back was ramrod straight and his shoulders were thrown back.

I shook off his hand. "What is it you want?" No matter how menacing Braden might look, the only danger he posed was that of talking a person to death.

"Aren't you worried I'll report you for consorting with the ladies?"

"*Consorting?*" I repeated, feeling only a little impressed that he'd conjured up such a large word. "Not particularly," I said, trying to sound uninterested. I turned away.

"I will!" he shouted after me, his voice shrill.

I stopped. He was just hysterical enough to cause problems. Maintaining my reputation and position in the household was one thing. Risking Lady Ariela's good name was another.

I turned to face him and lowered my voice. "Then what is it you want, boy?"

He winced at the slight on his age, but couldn't refute it. He was small in stature and, by my reckoning, wasn't a day over seventeen. Yet here he stood, threatening to reveal my secret like a youngster tattling on his older brother.

Braden stepped forward, laying hold of my arm again. "Please, Jonas, you have to help me."

I shook his grip off again and glared down at him, thinking of my youngest brother. Matthew would never dream of behaving like this. To do so would ensure a beating from all five of his elder brothers.

Correctly interpreting my expression as *Don't make me repeat myself*, or possibly *Keep your grubby paws off me*, Braden dropped his hands to his sides and made his request. "You must help me get close to Lady Larela."

At fifteen, Lady Larela was widely regarded as the most beautiful of the Earl of Bromhurst's daughters. In my estimation, she was nothing beside Ari. "And how do you propose I go about that? You know the rules."

He shifted from foot to foot. Even though he was rather new to the establishment, Gregor had painstakingly pounded the house rules into his head. *On pain of death*—I could practically see the words running through his mind. "She . . ." he hesitated, "she fancies me."

I snorted. "You mean you fancy her." The notion of the young lady sparing a thought for an impertinent, redheaded undergardener was laughable.

"Well, yes," he admitted. "But she fancies me as well. I've seen the way she looks at me when she passes."

I shook my head and considered the matter at hand. Larela was the most mischievous of Lord Bromhurst's daughters and the most difficult to keep in line. Lecture after lecture from her father on the subject of propriety hadn't prevented her from flirting with the young bucks among the staff. Mentioning this to Braden would probably only throw fuel on the fire of his passion. I had been that lovesick undergardener once. A seed of fellow-feeling nestled in my chest.

"Fine," I relented. "I'll speak to Lady Ariela when I have the chance. If she wants to, she can plead your case to her sister. I will promise nothing beyond that."

Braden looked pleased and took a step forward as if to embrace me.

"No." I held up a warning hand. The look on his face—the droop of a maltreated pooch—melted my resolve somewhat. I placed a hand on his shoulder. "May I give you some advice, Braden? Man to man?"

He perked up. If he'd had a tail, he'd have wagged it.

"Drop the theatrics." His brow darkened, but I

carried on just the same, determined to have my say. "Be a man. Not only will the others respect you for it, but your lady love," I almost choked on the words, "will take note as well."

"Thank you, Jonas. I'll do my best," he said, beaming up at me. "I'll make you proud." With that he strode off, head held high.

ℬℭ

Waltzing between flowerbeds and along grass-lined paths, I guided Ariela deeper into the flower garden. She looked up at me, her lashes dropping in the half-shy way that caused my heart to stutter. Caught in a bright beam of light, her skin appeared almost translucent, warmed only by pink spots high in her cheeks. Her lips curved up. The perfume of flowers pervaded the air, mingling with her scent. My heart soared as we danced for all the world to see, the full blooms nodding their approval. As one, our rhythm slowed, until once again she gazed up at me, trust and affection glowing in her eyes. Her lips parted as she spoke.

"Get up."

I looked quizzically down at her. The voice had been rough and gravelly.

"Get up." The words were more insistent this time. She took my shirt in two hands and shook me.

"Mmph?" I murmured incoherently, my eyes popping open to see not Ari's graceful long-fingered hands, but a set of hairy fists clutching my nightshirt.

They shook me so hard my teeth rattled.

"What's wrong with you, man? Didn't you hear the summons?"

I shook my head to dispel the last traces of the dream. Reality clicked into place as Gregor scowled down at me. I chided myself for dwelling on the impossible as I sat up, flung my legs out of bed, and rubbed my face one-handed. Gregor kicked my boots over to me.

"What's going on?" I asked as I shoved them on and grabbed my robe from its hook.

"It's the ladies of the house," he said. "They're missing."

My sleep-addled brain refused to process his words. "As in . . . missing?"

"Move, man!" he said, flinging open the door of the room we shared and flapping a hand to hustle me out.

"They're really gone?"

His mouth pulled into a grim line and his eyes narrowed in the dangerous way that meant someone was about to be sacked. Or smacked. "Now."

Forcing my sluggish brain into action, I made my way to the door and we started down the hall.

"Where have they gone?"

"That's what the entire staff's been driven from their beds to discover."

The sounds of shuffling feet met my ears. We fell into step with the other men headed toward the ballroom. I had rarely entered the chamber, and as we stepped inside, I took in the size of the room. The ballroom spanned half the length of the main house and rose two levels in height. The lower walls were covered with large mirrored panels and gilt sconces while a balcony ringed the upper level. Only a few of the sconces had been lit, leaving the room draped in shadow.

I spotted Lord Bromhurst at one end of the room, looking more disheveled than usual. The anxious maids and footmen fussing around him didn't improve his mood. We took our place at the opposite end of the room among those who were too lowly to claim a place near the Master and cluck over him. After a moment, the Earl of Bromhurst pushed away their anxious hands and stepped forward to address the whole group. "By now you'll have been informed that my daughters are missing."

Whispers ran through the group even though protocol called for complete silence during the His Lordship's speeches. I kept my eyes fixed on him, noting the stoop in his usually erect posture and the lines of exhaustion ringing his eyes.

Ari's words from the day before ran through my mind. He denied his children liberties and demanded they follow strict guidelines for behavior. Yet, as I watched him, sympathy pulled at my heart. He had already lost his wife. If something had befallen his daughters, he would be all alone.

He cleared his throat and the whispers ceased. "I entered their bedchamber to check on them an hour ago. We've been searching ever since. They are nowhere to be found."

A finger of worry tickled my spine. What had happened to the ladies? I remembered Ari's words. Her foolproof plan. What had she done?

"We have found no sign of them," the Master continued, running a hand through his hair in an uncharacteristic show of nervousness.

Between Ari's brilliance and Larela's ruthlessness, who knew what the sisters could have come up with or where they might have gone. Why had I allowed her to leave without telling me everything?

"After the death of my beloved wife . . ." Lord Bromhurst's voice faltered. "I needn't tell you how important it is that my daughters be found. Anyone with information regarding their whereabouts should come forward at once."

This was met with an uncomfortable silence as servants glanced at one another and squirmed self-consciously under the Master's eye. I half listened as the Earl called forward a number of the servants, Gregor among them, and proceeded to give them instructions on searching the grounds. I argued with myself, knowing I should speak up. I had very little of value to add. What if it meant nothing? I'd make matters worse for Ariela if I said too much.

Gregor returned to my side a moment later. The gardeners surrounded us, waiting for their assignments. I saw Gregor's mouth moving as he gave each of the men specific instructions, but the rushing in my ears covered the sound. If something had happened to Ari . .

"Jonas?" From the tone of his voice, he'd already said my name a number of times.

"Yes?" The word snapped out.

"We'll need torches. Take Loomis with you and bring as many as you can."

"Yes, sir." I spun away.

Gregor grabbed my elbow and leaned in to whisper, "Don't do anything stupid. Jonas. And for heaven's sake, keep an eye on Loomis. The last thing we need today is a fire."

I nodded curtly and pulled out of his grasp. Loomis lumbered alongside me. We reached the double doors leading out of the room. My mind raced ahead, trying to piece together everything Ariela had told me. My jaw clenched. If anyone had hurt her, I'd deal with them personally.

"Papa?" The word sounded from the upper level of the ballroom. High and bright, it rang over the nearly one hundred men and women in the room and cut through my rage. I hazarded a glance toward the balcony. Perched there in a long, white nightgown and rubbing the sleep from her eyes was the Master's youngest daughter.

"What is it?" Loomis mumbled.

I smacked him on the shoulder and pointed toward the upper level. The hubbub in the room subsided as others realized who had spoken.

"What's going on?" the young girl asked, her voice rusty from sleep.

"Larela?" Lord Bromhurst called out. "Where have you been?"

She yawned, covering her mouth with one hand. "In bed, Papa. Why is everyone up so early?"

The Earl pushed through the crowds to the staircase, his face stern. When he reached his daughter, he flung his arms around her, and spoke in tones too low to be heard. After a moment, he drew her to the edge of the balcony and faced us once more. All eyes were focused on the pair.

"Thank you, my friends. All of my daughters are accounted for. I thank you for your assistance." He squeezed Lady Larela's shoulders and the young girl winced. "We apologize for the inconvenience. I will personally see to it that nothing of the sort will happen in the future. You are excused."

The servants began to disperse, eager to return to their warm beds before they had to attend to the day's labors. Loomis, as impatient as the rest, tugged on my arm. I paid him no heed, my eyes fixed on the pair standing on the balcony. Lord Bromhurst's expression, mingled irritation and concern, was enough to reveal the gist of the lecture he imparted to his daughter. Lady Larela rubbed her eyes and yawned, looking younger than her fifteen years. After a time, the lines of concern on her father's brow relaxed and he towed her off.

Watching from below, something about the scene sat ill with me. Maybe it was my knowledge of the scheme Ari had concocted—however vague that knowledge might be. Maybe it was Lady Larela's eyes, which instead of being blurry with sleep, glowed with excitement like a cat that had lapped up a full saucer of cream. As they stepped out of view, something caught the light from a nearby sconce: the gleam of a gold dancing slipper disappearing beneath the hem of Lady Larela's nightdress.

Brisella

Returning to bed had been futile. Gregor's loud snoring and swine-like snuffling, along with the sight of that one gold slipper, drove sleep from my mind.

Lord Bromhurst's determination to separate his daughters from the outside world meant that visitors were rarely permitted and that the ladies were never allowed to leave the grounds unescorted. Regardless of his vigilance, they had slipped away. Someone had obviously helped them because dancing slippers weren't worn for one's own benefit.

I hoped for a meeting with Ari, and took special care in dressing, ensuring that my work clothes were clean and that my dark hair was combed into place. My own plain face stared back from the small mirror above the dresser. Tiny lines fanned out from sober eyes. The reflection declared that the time had come to search out a willing milkmaid or kitchen girl to bear me children and while away the years. But when I pictured the milkmaid, a grinning Ari appeared in servant's garb.

I rolled my eyes. The sentimental idiot in the mirror did the same.

ℰℭ

Punishment was today's theme. Aggravated by my recent behavior, Gregor had stripped me of my normal supervisory duties. When we reached the hedge that ringed the house, he frowned, mumbled some sort of threat, passed me a pair of hedge-clippers, and assigned me the task of trimming the section outside the drawing room window. Because it was set in full sun and far from the companionship of others, no one relished this particular task.

The summer heat intensified while I grumbled about the injustice of the world and battled the shrubbery. Sweat trickled down my back as morning gave way to early afternoon. I began to contemplate risking Gregor's wrath and skulking off to find lunch when movement on the other side of the window caught my attention. One glance through the glass confirmed the arrival of all twelve sisters, followed by their stern-looking father. Lord Bromhurst settled into a tall wingback chair beside the fireplace, while his daughters arranged themselves in twos and threes on the various settees and armchairs around the room. Several of them perched on the edge of the piano or leaned against the grandfather clock. The room, decorated in muted browns and reds and hung with a variety of family portraits, should have made a charming backdrop for a lovely scene between the girls and their father. However, the girls appeared uncharacteristically still, their youthful faces robbed of smiles.

"Heavens this room is warm!" a voice declared from the other side of the glass. Lady Larela, her blonde curls bouncing, cast me a mischievous half-grin and flung up the window. Between the grin and the dimple creasing her cheek, I could understand why so many fancied her.

"Come away from there, child," her father ordered.

Her green eyes twinkled and she dropped me a wink before obeying her father. I looked away and busied myself with the job at hand, careful to keep the hedge between me and the window, but listening closely just the same.

"Now, ladies," their father intoned, "What do you have to say for yourselves?"

Twelve voices, from soprano to alto, sounded at once. The Master cleared his throat, and like the servants had done the night before, the sisters fell silent. "One at a time, if you please." This was probably accompanied by the same glare he bent on servants who had displeased him. "Ariela, you may begin."

My ears strained for the sound of her voice.

"It's just as Lari told you, Father. We were in our bedchamber all night." The lie was so fluid I almost believed it myself.

"Perhaps you had a nightmare, Father." That was Lady Brisella, piping up in support of Ari. They were born allies.

31

"Oh, yes, Father."

"A nightmare."

"Couldn't have been anything else." Several voices chimed in at the same time.

"That's all you have to say for yourselves?"

I peeked in the window. Sure enough, Lord Bromhurst's lips were drawn into a grim line. That expression alone usually prompted a confession.

Lady Canela flipped her red hair over her shoulder and narrowed her hazel eyes. "Perhaps you had too much wine last night." *Cinnamon*, her sisters nicknamed her, was unafraid of saying what she thought. Even to her father.

His expression turned so thunderous that steam practically poured from his ears.

Lady Brisella went to his side, laying a hand on his shoulder. "None of us really believe that, Father."

"Then what?" he asked crossly. "I *dreamed* I entered your bedchamber and found nothing but empty beds?"

When Lady Brisella's calm demeanor couldn't reach her father, Ari knelt beside his chair and took his hand in both of hers. "It's a simple misunderstanding, Father. That's all." Her words were so soft, so true, they couldn't fail to move him.

The Master's eyes hardened, snapping with fury. With one hand he none-too-gently grasped Ariela's chin. Ari, her actions and emotions controlled at all times, winced. It was all I could do to keep from leaping over the hedge and bounding through the window to wrench her from his hold.

"Then I will make this simple, my child. This is the last time you'll make a fool of me." Malice laced the words.

No longer pretending to sculpt the hedge, I leaned closer to catch his next remark.

"It is past time you found homes of your own. As soon as I can arrange it, I will find husbands for all of you."

The statement was met with silence.

"Do you understand?"

Ari, her chin still in his palm, nodded, her eyes glossy with unshed tears.

"Good," he replied, releasing her and turning to look over the rest of his daughters. "In the meantime, footmen will be placed outside your rooms at night to ensure you comport yourself as befits ladies of your station."

The girls stared back at him, their faces showing everything from disbelief to defiance.

He stood and brushed off his suit coat, as if brushing off the unpleasant scene that had played out. "Good day, ladies," he said, striding out of the room.

A few timid voices called, "Good day, Father." Most of the girls remained silent, waiting for Brisella to close the door before speaking.

"What are we to do?" several ladies queried at once.

"We'll do exactly what we've been doing," Canela said, her voice as hard as her father's had been. "He can't stop us."

"It's not worth the risk." Brisella said. Her eyes pleaded with Ari, who still sat beside the chair their father had vacated. I watched as she took a bracing breath and swept a hand over her eyes.

She tipped her face up to meet Brisella's gaze. "First things first." She rose from her place on the floor and moved toward the window.

Toward me.

Her hand slipped into her pocket, emerging with a tiny scrap of paper clutched between two fingers. She paused when she reached the windowsill. I wanted to ask if she was all right and assure her of my protection in time of need. Something in her golden eyes, the way they shone brighter than usual, like she was on the verge of tears, stilled my tongue. Her mouth pulled into a line and she slid the window closed and pulled the heavy drapes shut, blocking my vision of the room and its occupants.

Lost in concern for the ladies' welfare, I almost forgot the bit of paper lying on the windowsill. Creased into a square, it looked inconsequential. I snatched it up and rubbed it between my fingers, like a child savoring a gift and guessing what it might contain.

I dropped down between the hedge and the building, eased it open, and read:

Ruins, 2:00

-A

Simple as the missive was, it pleased me that she had thought to pen it. Had she known her father would launch a full interrogation? Even if she had, she never could have guessed I'd be stationed nearby. She must have prepared the note in case our paths crossed.

The thought of speaking with Ari raised my spirits. She would explain what she and her sisters had been up to, and as always, I would listen and counsel her to the best of my abilities. The pattern was familiar. Comfortable.

I recalled our first meeting at the ruins a dozen years earlier. The promises of girlhood were fulfilled in the woman Ariela had become. I often felt like the awkward farm boy of yesteryear, but at least I had learned to speak to women instead of mutely gawp at them. Over the years, gentlemen had come and gone and offers for Ari's hand had been made. Ariela had shown little or no interest in the prospect of marriage and had never accepted. For his own reasons, her father hadn't forced the matter until now.

As the loud clock on the other side of the glass struck two, I laid aside the gardening tools to make my way to the ruins.

I slowed my pace and quieted my thoughts as I approached our meeting place. It always pleased me to come upon Ari and catch sight of her silhouette—the smooth line of cheek, the determined chin, the glint of cleverness in her eye—before she was aware of my presence. The sight that met me today disconcerted more than pleased me. The slim woman wasn't reading or gazing into the distance while she hatched a plan; instead, she paced the length of the cracked stone floor. Back and forth, back and forth.

"Ariela?" I called out uncertainly.

"Do you have any idea how long I've been waiting?"

It could be no more than five minutes past the hour as the walk from the house to the ruins took no longer than that. I was on the verge of pointing this out when I noted her quivering chin.

"Stop looking at me like that, Jonas!" She perched on a crumbling chunk of wall, wrapped her arms around herself, and frowned at a piece of broken masonry.

If Loomis or Braden had spoken to me in the same way I would have been annoyed. This display—so uncharacteristic of Ariela—alarmed me.

Without another thought, I settled at her side. "What is it, Ari?"

Wearily, she swiped a hand over her face. "You heard him, Jonas. He's going to sell us off to the highest bidder."

I blinked. "That seems a bit vulgar."

"You know what I mean," she responded, tilting her tear-stained face up to me. "My father will pass me off to the first eligible bachelor he can find."

"It's nothing he hasn't mentioned before."

"Yes, but today he meant it." A trickle of tears ran down her cheek.

I recalled the rough way her father had taken her chin in his hand and the cold words he had spoken. I couldn't shake the image from my mind or the anger that made my stomach churn. Without thinking, I put an arm around her shoulder. She released a great sob and buried her face in my chest. I wrapped my arms around her and held her as she cried, trying all the while to ignore how glorious it felt. After a minute or two, I fished a crumpled handkerchief out of my pocket and pressed it into her hand.

She let out half a chuckle at its wrinkled state and pulled away to swab at her face. "I'm sorry, Jonas. I shouldn't have been so short-tempered."

I shrugged. "We were due for a good quarrel."

She let out a snuffly laugh. "It's not even your fault." She swiped at her nose. "I'm sorry I was cross. I've never been treated like that by my father."

"I know," I said, taking the handkerchief from her to dab at the last of the moisture on her face. I tried not to think about the intimacy of the gesture or how easy it would be to cup her cheek in my palm. "If you'd just accepted one of the young dukes or lordlings who'd come calling, we wouldn't be in this mess."

"If any of them had possessed half the natural kindness and good sense you do, Jonas, I might have," she said.

The implication hung in the air between us. I wondered idly if she'd mind becoming a milkmaid.

"You've been nothing but wonderful to me and look how I've treated you. Can you forgive me?"

I nodded once, banishing the image of Ari in milkmaid's garb for the second time that day. "Already done."

A miserable little smile curved her mouth. She rested her head on my shoulder. Focusing on the way her body felt pressed against mine would turn my mind to liquid and any chance of offering help would be swallowed up in my need to . . . but I couldn't afford to think about that. Especially not now.

"What will we do?" she asked.

I thanked the heavens for her words, which distracted me from treading into dangerous territory. I could fix problems, I told myself. It was my role in our relationship.

"What are you thinking?"

"I think it was a mistake to start this whole venture," she said flatly. "Now that we're in this deep, I don't know if there's a way back."

I wanted to ask what she meant, but I reminded myself it was her questions we were addressing and not mine. I chose only the most innocent of queries. "Why not?"

She turned those lovely eyes on me, now red-rimmed and showing signs of exhaustion. "We've had a taste of freedom, Jonas. Do you think we can walk away from it?"

My curiosity flared up again. I bottled it up with an effort. "Is it safe?"

She let out a rueful laugh. "Is anything beyond your own front door safe?" Thoughtfulness settled over her features and she seemed to calm somewhat. "For that matter, much that happens behind closed doors can be dangerous. Lari, for instance, can do serious damage with an embroidery needle."

I chuckled. "Then what will you do?"

She sniffed and then wiped her nose. "Carry on, I suppose, if we can manage it. If the Duke's son can do it—"

Her comment caught me off-guard. "Who?"

"Oh you know, the Duke of Trentwich, whose heir escaped all responsibility and is now living on some tropical island and having a perfectly wonderful time. Or at least that's what they say."

I'd heard nothing of the duke's runaway heir and cared little for someone so spoiled and entitled. The bravado of Ari's words didn't distract me from the sadness in her eyes. A small smudge remained on her cheek, and without thinking, I rubbed a thumb over it. I froze, my hand cupping her cheek. Shyly, she looked up at me through tear-matted lashes. My mind froze. I knew no more than that moment—my hand on her damp cheek, and her trusting gaze holding mine.

With great effort I pulled my hand away and forced out the words, "You know I'll help you however I can. I can't provide endless fortune and a tropical island, but if a remote farm is what you want—"

She caught my hand between hers and pressed it tightly. "You'd move heaven and earth to take me there? I know, Jonas."

She'd said it so flippantly. If only she knew the truth of the sentiment. Thoughts flashed through my mind. Should I tell her? Should I confess that moving heaven and earth was a small price to pay if her love were the reward? The words hovered on the tip of my tongue. I opened my mouth.

She gave my hand another squeeze. "I will always be grateful for your friendship."

Canela

The young woman leaned against the squared stones of the big house and bent all her charms—scads of red curls pouring over her shoulders and curves indecent anywhere outside of a brothel—on the manservant before her.

As I shaped a nearby shrubbery, I watched the interchange and almost felt sorry for the manservant. When Lady Canela set a plan in action, she could not be distracted before its completion. The look on the servant's face—somewhere between village idiot and lovesick teenager—guaranteed she'd get whatever she wanted out of him.

She placed a hand on his chest and gazed up at him through long lashes. What could she possibly be telling him? Tilting my head to the side, I tried to catch the last few words of their conversation. I heard nothing more than the buttery murmur of Canela's voice. If the bobbing of her companion's head was anything to go

41

by, he'd just vowed to give his dying breath to fulfill her wishes. I examined the shrubbery—it would be a good place to vomit.

Canela sashayed off, rewarding her victim with a lingering look at her retreating hips before she disappeared around the corner of the building. The whole scene left me uneasy. And slightly ill. Canela was by far the most ruthless of the sisters. If a way to escape their confinement had been discovered, she would be the last to abandon the plan.

I resolved to keep an eye on the servant. At present, he stood with his mouth gaping like a landed trout, staring at the place where Canela had been. He would be of no use to me until he recovered himself. I worked over the shrubbery while I contemplated the situation.

Canela's was the first suspicious behavior I had witnessed in days. For a week, the sisters had played the role of model daughters and followed their father's counsel by engaging in the feminine pursuits of embroidery, music, and garden rambles. As he had vowed, their father had posted guards by their rooms at night and had arranged visits from several landed and titled gentlemen. The first of many—Lord Something-or-other—would arrive that afternoon.

I turned my attention back to the servant Canela had addressed and willed him into action. Nothing happened. His mind was undoubtedly lost to thoughts of the lady in question in various compromising positions. Would it be impolite to lob a branch at his head to remind him of his duty?

Minutes ticked by while the servant stared into space. The bush I trimmed diminished in size. I assessed the damage. There would be no way to hide this from Gregor unless I could convince Loomis to uproot it before Gregor saw it. Again.

As if thinking of the Devil could conjure him, I heard Gregor berating a nearby gardener. The noise seemed to bring Lady Canela's devotee to his senses. He glanced back and forth and darted off as soon as he heard the commotion. I skirted along the edge of the main building, careful to keep him in sight while keeping Gregor a safe distance behind. As I crept around the corner of the house, a bellow sounded.

Gregor had discovered my handiwork. By the sound of it, he was duly impressed. Nothing could be done now. Gregor would have to wait until later to share his thoughts on my shrubbery-shaping skills.

I followed the servant past the house to the kitchen gardens. Ordinarily, gardeners tending the plants or scullery maids gathering things for the kitchen occupied the area. At the moment, they stood empty.

The servant looked about once again. Before he caught sight of me, I ducked behind a nearby bush. He must not have detected the movement, for the man ventured forward, stooping to finger and sniff various plants. He uprooted one plant with pale pink blossoms and plucked leaves from another before tucking them into an inner pocket. I watched him leave, more curious about the herbs he had gathered than his final destination.

Had Canela tasked him with collecting *herbs*? Everything in her attitude indicated that this task was important. Why would a woman go to such lengths for leaves?

"Suspicious behavior," a voice beside me spoke, freezing me in place. Crouched behind the bush, I fixed my eyes on the heavy-soled boots planted in front of me. With growing dread, my eyes traveled up the brown-trousered legs, past the brown apron and white shirt, and finally to his face. It sported the displeased expression I expected.

I sighed in relief just the same.

"It seems you're always up to something, Jonas," Braden said, his eyes narrowed to slits. "Spying on the women, are we?"

With an inward sigh, I pushed myself to a standing position and looked down my nose at him. Though I had been the one caught skulking behind the bushes, his holier-than-thou demeanor bothered me. "And if I was, what business is it of yours?"

The displeasure on his face intensified. "In case you hadn't noticed, they are noblewomen. As such—"

I was unimpressed by his newfound loyalty to the upper class. I stopped him by raising one hand and focused on making my tone calm before I spoke. "Do you see any ladies nearby, Braden?"

He glanced about, possibly wondering if I had secreted them behind another bush. Unable to detect even the slightest hint of a woman, Braden shrugged.

"Then, if you'll leave me be," I said, turning to

stride through the kitchen gardens, "I have matters to attend to."

"In the kitchen gardens? If you'd been stationed here, I'd know about it."

I stopped, struck by my own foolishness. For a few weeks now, this had been Braden's assignment. He took the responsibility seriously and knew I didn't belong here. "I'm inspecting the plants in Gregor's behalf." It was a plausible lie since I held the title of second-in-command in everything but name. I bent to rub at the leaves the servant had gathered. A lemon scent with a mint undertone wafted through the air.

"Why would he ask you to do that?" Braden demanded.

"Maybe he feels the work being done here is unacceptable."

Braden didn't back down. "Then I'll have to speak with him about it myself," he said, turning to go. The glint in his eye told me he knew he had called my bluff.

"Wait," I called after him. The only person Gregor found more annoying than Loomis was Braden. And possibly me, at the moment. "That's not necessary."

He turned back. "Then tell me what you are really doing."

"Fine," I sighed, resigned, though I wouldn't mention Lady Canela's part in things. His jab about spying on the ladies had fallen too close to the mark.

"A moment ago, there was a suspicious-looking servant gathering plants here. I wondered what he was up to."

"*Another* suspicious-looking servant?"

I tried not to roll my eyes at the insinuation. If he carried on like this, I would offer no further explanation and make a point of ignoring him in the future. I was about to leave when he spoke.

"Which plants was he looking at?"

I indicated a plant like the one the servant had uprooted as well as the minty plant I'd been fingering.

"Valerian and lemon balm," he muttered. Braden's brow knit together while he thought. "That's rather a strong combination."

"What do you mean?" I asked, suddenly very interested in what he had to say.

"Well," he shrugged, "the combination could be made into a sleeping draft. Paired with alcohol, it would be pretty potent."

I mulled this over for a minute, wondering why Canela would require such a powerful combination. "Thank you, Braden." I prepared to leave. "This has been quite . . ." I struggled for a word that wouldn't make him bounce about like a young pup, "helpful."

The last of the storm cloud vanished from his face. I flinched at the shower of appreciation that would surely be forthcoming. He surprised me by only saying, "My pleasure, Jonas."

Maybe he was learning to control his emotions at last. One could only hope.

I nodded in reply and made to step past him out of the gardens, but with a quick sideways movement, Braden blocked my path.

"And now," he said, "it's your turn to help me."

I should have guessed this was coming. No wonder he had behaved with restraint.

"You will arrange for a private reunion with Larela as soon as possible."

"Nonsense," I replied. "You know it isn't allowed. Anyone caught alone with the Master's daughters could be discharged."

"And yet," he added, "that has never stopped *you*."

The urge to throw him into the closest bush—preferably something with thorns—was difficult to curb. "I agreed to speak to Lady Ariela about the matter, and that is all I will do." I too could be determined. I wasn't the eldest of six brothers for nothing.

"That was before I was so helpful to you. And before I saw the very servant you referred to speaking with Lady Canela. I'm sure Gregor would love to hear about it."

I should have thrown him into a thorny bush when I had the chance. Ariela and her sisters were in enough trouble without adding illicit interludes with servants to the list of their misdeeds.

"I'll just be working over there," he motioned to the farthest corner of the garden plot, "if you need me. Please inform me when my meeting with Larela will take place."

I watched him go, hating him a little more with each self-satisfied step he took. No servant had the right to act so haughty.

୫୬୯

A carriage—black, silver, and superior-looking—swept up the drive in an elegant arc. The man inside was probably accustomed to trumpet fanfares marking his arrival, for when the door opened and the stairs were let down, he waited an extra thirty seconds before stepping out. He was as black, silver, and superior-looking as the carriage, with knee boots shined to a high gloss, dark hair slicked off his square brow, and a finely cut black suit trimmed in silver. Overall, he emitted an air of wealth.

The servants, arranged in a line in front of the manor, had a perfect view of the honored guest as he strode forward. From the far left, I watched him step up to the Master and look over Ariela and her sisters appraisingly. The thought of rushing forward and flattening him into the cobbled drive and the subsequent satisfaction I would feel filled my mind. My fists clenched in anticipation.

He swept a low bow, taking the opportunity to glance down the line of ladies again. From where I stood, I could see the pleasure in his face at being presented with such an overabundance of beauty.

It would be so easy to pummel him into submission. He'd never expect an attack from the household staff. I pressed my fists to my sides and planted my feet in place instead.

"Viscount Mansbury," Lord Bromhurst intoned, bowing in return. "Welcome to our humble home." He gestured with a wave of his hand. "May I present my daughters?" At the introduction of each girl, Lord Mansbury stepped up to her, paused to press a kiss to her hand, and treated her to a smoldering glance. I wondered how Lady Larela felt having his lips pressed to her hand and being treated to the same calculated expression that had been given to her eleven older sisters. If the curl of her lip and the arch of her brow were any indication, Larela found the moment less than enjoyable. She reminded me of my youngest brother, Matthew, who felt the same way about his brothers' castoffs. No one hated hand-me-downs more than he.

Looking down the line of servants, I noted delight on the faces of the women and more than one man with a grim expression. Perhaps I wasn't the only man who didn't idolize nobility. I glanced down the line to catch Braden's reaction, but couldn't see him.

After Mansbury had greeted Lady Larela, he stepped back to address the company. "I thank you, Lord Bromhurst for your warm welcome," his voice was higher than I expected. "I look forward to furthering our acquaintance."

With a stony expression, Lord Bromhurst took Ari's arm and said, "Shall we step inside for some refreshment?" Two footmen scuttled forward to swing open the heavy double doors. The Master led the procession indoors.

Lord Mansbury lost no time in offering an arm each to Brisella and Canela, the latter—whom I expected to snub him—graced him with her most winning smile and took his arm. Lady Brisella responded with less enthusiasm as she took her place on his other side. Trailing behind the trio, the rest of the ladies fell into line without a word, communicating with each other only in fleeting looks.

My gratitude toward Lord Bromhurst for appropriating Ari's arm was immense. Could it be his way of expressing his disapproval of Lord Mansbury?

A hand squeezing my shoulder brought an end to my musings. "What do you make of him?" Braden asked in a carrying whisper. Given the murderous look Gregor sent our way, everyone had heard it.

With a shove, I pushed Braden away from the group of servants. The tight line of servants had begun to break up as everyone returned to their work.

I raised an eyebrow and glared down at Braden. "Do you want to get us both sacked?"

"No, I—"

"Then keep your comments to yourself." Concern for Ari and her sisters, along with the desire to help them without losing my position, occupied my thoughts most of the time. Why did I have to tolerate his loose tongue too?

Braden's eyes flashed and his jaw clenched, but he made no reply.

I ignored his silence and continued to chastise him the same way he had chastised me earlier. "You can't blurt out whatever comes to mind, Braden. Especially when it concerns your betters."

His eyes lost some of their snap. "I apologize if I

misspoke."

"You should probably see to your duties now."

Without arguing and with less buoyancy that usual, he departed. I watched him and considered the question he'd asked. Though I might refuse to admit it to Braden, I had already begun sizing up Lord Mansbury. He was handsome and titled—something the Master valued in a prospective suitor—but was he worthy? His carefully styled hair and the expensive cut of his suit spoke more of vanity than of intellect and good nature.

As afternoon gave way to evening, I wondered what Ari would make of him. Would she consider him a worthy companion for her future life? Or would she accept his hand and a share of his fortune and consider that enough? Only time would tell.

Daniela

"He's gone."

I raised an eyebrow.

"Lord Mansbury," Gregor explained when he saw my confusion. "He left this morning."

"Really?" I asked, failing to hide my eagerness. To cover it, I added, "He just arrived yesterday. What happened?"

"No one knows. However, the Master's mood is especially dark this morning."

"Darker than usual?"

Gregor's eyes narrowed, daring me to ask another question. "The morning is wasting away, Jonas. If you'd like breakfast, we need to get moving."

More questions sprang to my lips. I bit my tongue and followed him down to the kitchen. Gregor might be less than forthcoming, but someone would be willing to offer up the information I needed.

The maids' excited buzzing could be heard from the

corridor outside the servants' dining area. Snippets of their conversation—words like "shocking behavior," and "scandal"—reached my ear. My mind filled with scenarios that could have resulted in Mansbury's early removal from the manor. I favored those that included him falling from the second floor and breaking various body parts. Like his neck.

We stepped into the room and the gossip mill ground to a halt. I should have known Gregor's sober presence would have this effect. I looked from one tight-lipped maid to another and my fears were confirmed. No one here would tell me anything. I'd just have to find another way to discover what had happened.

୫୬

Through a fair amount of finagling, I earned a post in the flower garden for the afternoon. I didn't escape without a glare from Gregor and a lecture on attending to my duties and nothing else. It was a small price to pay. The flower garden was the best place to gather intelligence on the comings and goings in the big house. Ladies' maids could be interrogated when they arrived to gather bouquets for the manor. Since Gregor would be nowhere nearby, the women would be more willing to tell me what had occurred.

Unlike the herb garden, the flower garden was laid out in a pinwheel with trim paths winding out from the middle. The center of the garden, set with wrought iron benches, chairs, and small tables, was ringed by a wall of rosebushes thick enough to offer privacy to those who sought it.

I trimmed hedges and watched carefully for the maids. No one arrived. They had apparently made their trips to the flower garden before my arrival. As the sun made its final steps toward the west, I gave up all hope of learning about the viscount's departure until later. Then the sound of several sets of footsteps on cobblestones met my ears. I glanced up, my hopes rising with the sight of the Master's daughters heading down the garden paths in duos and trios. After the last sister had passed, I made sure that Gregor wasn't nearby and that nosy Braden was nowhere to be seen. Then, I followed the women into the heart of the garden, making sure I stayed behind the vegetation.

The ladies were already deep in conversation when I took my place on the other side of the rose hedge.

"He deserved it." The voice brimmed with the type of indignation only the very young can muster. Lady Larela, no doubt.

"Don't be so hasty, Lari," the much more reticent Daniela cautioned, her voice barely carrying beyond the rose hedge.

"Yes," Canela agreed with a note of sarcasm. "He only meant to carry one of us off and set us to baby-making."

Shocked silence met the proclamation. Though the comment struck uncomfortably close to the truth, I slapped a hand over my mouth to hold back a chuckle. I imagined the sisters glancing at one another with wide eyes and open mouths.

"He's gone. That's what's important." Even if I hadn't immediately recognized the voice, the logic of the statement would still have convinced me that it was Ariela.

"True," her youngest sister agreed. With a titter, she added, "and wasn't it lovely to see him go?"

More chuckles and giggles.

"It was genius, Bree," Canela complimented her sister.

"What was genius?" someone else asked.

I could sense Brisella's discomfort from my hiding place.

"I had little to do with it. It was Daniela and Janela, really," she said, attempting to deflect attention from herself. As usual.

Daniela's voice, soft as a breeze, floated over her sisters' chatter. "Our concoction would have done little without your intervention."

"Concoction?"

"Intervention?"

"It sounds gross."

I didn't recognize the voices, but it might have been the triplets. They interrupted, contradicted, and talked over one another every time they opened their mouths.

"Tell them how you did it," Larela begged, like a little girl asking for her favorite bedtime story. Skirts and shoes shuffled as the ladies settled in to listen.

Finally, I thought, leaning forward.

Brisella let out a soft sigh. "All right," she relented,

uncomfortable with so much attention. "Everything fell together when we met Mansbury yesterday. He smelled strongly of alcohol." Brisella continued, "Janela and Daniela had been studying . . ." This was met with several murmurs, but no surprise. The two sisters, though separated by several years, gravitated toward one another because of their shared love of books and learning. "They found an ancient volume on remedies for illnesses, and as you know, they began experimenting with several of them."

The sisters snickered. I felt like I had missed something important. I hadn't heard anything about the sisters' experiments. I leaned further into the hedge to catch every word of explanation.

Lady Brisella carried on. "They discovered a collection of herbs that, when combined in the correct quantities with alcohol, renders the drinker senseless for several hours."

"Dani thought it might be of use if Father stationed trustworthy guards at our door," Lady Janela explained, "the kind that can't be bribed into silence."

"It could still happen," Lady Daniela said softly. "We've been lucky so far, but who knows when that might change."

"You needn't worry so much," Lady Canela said. "Most men are susceptible to either bribery or flattery." She continued, "Would you be so kind as to finish the story, Bree?"

"Of course. Do you all remember the pungent smell hanging about the stairwell last week?" Muttered assent greeted Brisella's question. "That was the first of Janela and Dani's experiments."

"Is that what it was?"

"I was sure something had died."

"Completely disgusting."

My mouth formed an O. The servants had smelled it from the other side of the manor. We assumed something had happened in the kitchen to create what Braden had described as the "stink of unwashed underthings and dead animals." No wonder the cooks and scullery maids had been indignant at the accusations.

"So," Brisella continued, "I bribed one of our manservants to offer Lord Mansbury a nightcap when he retired for the evening. And he informed Lord Mansbury we would be waiting to toast to our future happiness in our personal chambers."

Janela joined in the tale. "Canela persuaded our guards to make themselves scarce for a quarter of an hour. And when Mansbury arrived, Brisella offered to refill his glass and added a healthy dose of our mixture to his drink."

I drew back in surprise and immediately entangled myself in the hedge. I struggled to free myself from the thorns and hoped the girls would pay no heed to the rustling.

"What's that?" Larela called out.

"Probably just one of the feral cats."

"Ew! Cats!"

"Calm down!" Canela snapped. More coolly, she

said, "By the way Bree, you're not telling it right. Would you care to finish it, Dani?"

I pictured Daniela's shy smile as she stepped to the forefront. Softly, she said, "He never would have taken it from me. But he already had his eye on Bree, so we thought she was best suited for the job. No one would suspect her of doing anything underhanded."

I listened to the ladies' good-natured laughter and used the extra noise to free myself from the thorns. I inspected the new tear in my sleeve and the long scratch beneath it that began to bleed while I considered what they'd said. Scheming fell squarely in Ari's camp, while unseemly behavior fell to Canela, Larela, or the triplets. No one would assume Brisella would have anything to do with questionable deeds. Like drugging a visiting nobleman.

"I suspect you've been watching me for years, Bree," Canela said airily. "I'd never seen that combination of batted lashes and shy blushing before. The man didn't stand a chance."

The girls laughed again, Brisella's soft laughter joining in with the rest.

"Tell them what happened next, Dani," Larela pressed.

"Yes, please!" the others added.

"All right," Daniela relented, picking up the thread of the story. "Within moments of taking the drink, Mansbury passed out cold. Right there in the hallway."

"At which point we dragged him into our sitting room and propped him up on the couch," Brisella added. Snickers met this comment.

"Then *someone*," Ari's voice rose a notch above the rest, "sloshed gin all over him."

"We had to make the ruse complete," Canela explained, without a hint of embarrassment.

"Or Father would never have believed Lord Mansbury had done something as improper as enter our rooms unescorted," Larela added.

I left off dabbing at the cut on my arm to peer through the leaves. The sisters were positively diabolical. Luckily, I had brothers instead.

"You have to admit it was effective. When our guards informed Father that Lord Mansbury had made his way into our private rooms, the look on his face must have been positively murderous," Canela said.

"It certainly was when he arrived," Larela said. "And he blamed Mansbury entirely."

"It didn't hurt that when the Viscount came to, he muttered, 'Mighty fine wenches, Bromhurst!'" Canela added, affecting a low, manly tone.

The inner garden rang with laughter. I shook my head, hardly believing it possible they had taken such action. At the same time, I couldn't help feeling relief that Lord Mansbury would never be permitted to return.

"How did I sleep through all of that?" one of the triplets complained.

"How do you think we knew the concoction worked?" Canela replied archly. Her sisters burst into roars of laughter that lasted for the better part of a minute.

"Much as I admire your cleverness," Ari's serious tone cut through the mirth, "we cannot dose every lord that comes our way. Sooner or later, we'll be found out." The sisters' merriment was cut short and replaced by an uncomfortable silence. "Then, our midnight excursions will have to come to an end."

Midnight excursions, the phrase rattled around my mind. Would this be the moment that I would discover what those excursions entailed? I resisted the urge to look at her through the bushes. Those thorns were unforgiving.

Brisella broke the silence. "We will cross that bridge when we come to it, Ariela."

"Yes," Daniela agreed, "we'll find the solution together."

This group of women, thrown together by birth and tied by bonds of friendship, never ceased to amaze me. They might be different in coloring and temperament, but together they were virtually unstoppable. My heart panged as I thought of how quickly a bond like theirs could be severed by a change in circumstances. The close comradeship I shared with my brothers was similar. When the opportunity for a better job arose, I had no choice but to leave them behind. If Lord Bromhurst had his way, the same would occur within his household. As his elder daughters were sent to homes of their own, the sisters would part and live separate lives.

The meeting broke up while dark thoughts cluttered my mind. Once again in twos and threes, the ladies made their way out of the garden. Most of the girls had passed my hiding place when Brisella, Daniela, and Janela breezed by. Ari trailed a few paces behind them, her eyes downcast and concern furrowing her brow.

My heart brimmed with sorrow for all that would befall Ariela and her sisters. As she passed, I reached out a hand, grasped hers, and pulled her behind the rose hedge. Taken off-guard, she bumped into my chest with a quick intake of breath. Her scent filled my nostrils and my eyes dwelled on her pink lips, parted in surprise. Her warm breath mingled with mine.

When I tore my eyes from her lips, I noted that the tiny furrow between her eyebrows had deepened. I blinked, took a step back, and dropped her hand.

Ariela's mouth snapped closed. "How much did you hear?"

I didn't say a thing.

"Then there's nothing left for me to say." She turned away, leaving me with no more than a partial view of her profile.

"Ari, please."

She released a sigh, weariness lining the shadows of her face.

"You said it yourself, Ari. This ruse can't go on forever."

She folded her arms tightly as if trying to hold herself together.

I took a step toward her. "However this ends, I will do all I can to protect you from the aftermath."

She turned back to me, the sorrow and anger in her

expression fading. Then she noticed the tear in my sleeve. "What have you done, Jonas?"

"It's nothing." I clapped my palm over the blood-streaked fabric.

Gently, she peeled my fingers away and moved the material aside to look at the wound beneath it. "Oh, Jonas. I'm so sorry."

The softness of her fingertips unnerved me. Gentleness encouraged any number of inappropriate ideas. Her anger was preferable.

"It's nothing. Really," I repeated.

"Promise you'll have it seen to?"

I nodded.

The gravity in her eyes eased and one corner of her mouth curved up before the other joined it. Her hand moved to cup my cheek. "Jonas, what would I do without you?" My heart stuttered to a stop. I froze in place, not daring to imagine what would happen next. Standing on tiptoe, Ari brushed a kiss across the other cheek and whispered, "Thank you," before she left me alone on the garden path.

The interchange replayed in my mind long after Ari's scent had faded away. I wanted to fix everything, but how could I help her when my wits abandoned me in her presence? Suddenly an image of the love-struck servant Canela had charmed came to mind. I was no different from him and would be just as incapable of independent thought if I didn't learn to master my emotions.

If Ariela and her sisters weren't already in over

their heads, they soon would be. I had to discover how they escaped each night and what activities they participated in once they did. Given her present mood, tagging after Ariela and begging for the truth would be fruitless. For now, I had to figure out how to learn more on my own.

ഇൗരു

"They say the gentlemen are ever so handsome," the maid said as she tucked into her breakfast.

"Indeed, anyone with *that* yearly income must be attractive," her companion giggled.

From the next table over, I rolled my eyes and poked at my porridge with my spoon. I could never keep the names of all of the maids straight. Dressed alike in their plain black dresses and crisp white aprons, they all blended together. Much like the porridge before me—always the same color, consistency, and bland flavor. I prodded at it again before lifting a spoonful to my mouth.

"Do you think the ladies will fancy them?" the first maid asked, leaning closer to her friend.

"They'd be fools not to," the other replied. "Sons of an earl. Titled, landed, and connected to everyone of importance. What more could they want?"

A logical question. But, so far money, land, and good breeding hadn't been enough of an enticement for any of Bromhurst's daughters. Would their acquaintance with the next two noblemen, set to arrive within hours, have a different outcome?

"The ladies are nothing if not particular," the first maid said, shaking her head in disapproval.

"True," the other agreed. "Though the heavens only know why."

The maids were simple girls with humble beginnings like my own among folk who knew little more than the meaning of a good living. They dreamed of being set up for life in a fine home and prosperous lands but would ultimately settle for something far less grand.

Year after year, Ari and her sisters had rejected one suitor after another. Like the maids, part of me would never understand their choice to remain single. If they had been born farmer's daughters, they wouldn't have been able to imagine rejecting an offer of marriage from an eligible gentleman.

"We'll know by evening if they've changed their tune," the first maid said, pulling me back to their conversation.

"Or if the Master's changed it for them," her companion added, with a tilt of her head.

My spoon slipped out of my hand and clanked against the bottom of my bowl. Both girls scowled at me. I cleared my throat. Quickly, I stood and swept up my dishes. Their glares bored into my back until I left the room.

I let out a sigh of relief and headed outdoors. I scanned the grounds for Gregor and found him standing by a bow-shouldered undergardener. When I drew nearer, I caught Gregor's words.

"How many times must I tell you? That is a *bush*, Loomis, not a weed!"

Beside their feet, I caught a glimpse of an upturned bush, its roots waving surrender.

Loomis looked sheepish.

"And on today of all days!" Gregor blustered.

Loomis muttered an apology. I remembered what I had done to a bush the day before and stopped in my tracks. Slowly, I began to back away. I could approach Gregor to get my assignment another time.

"Too late, Jonas!" Gregor bellowed, pinning me in place.

I probably looked like an idiot with one foot hanging in midair. I dropped it to the ground. "Anything I can do to help?"

"After yesterday's antics, the least you can do is help Loomis repair the damage he has done."

"Of course, Gregor." I bowed my head. "It would be my pleasure."

"I'll leave you to it." Gregor looked back and forth between Loomis and me. "Between the two of you, I expect you'll find some way to muck it up."

"Just a hint," I said when Gregor was safely out of earshot. "That part," I nudged the roots with the toe of my boot, "goes in the ground."

೫೦೦೪

With the bush replanted the right way up, it looked as if it might survive. I tamped one last layer of soil around the slim trunk. Rapid footsteps sounded behind me.

"Jonas," Gregor said, between gasps of breath. "They've arrived early. Round up as many gardeners as you can and have them report at the front entrance." His jaw was tight and a sheen of sweat shone on his brow.

"Right away," I said, standing up and brushing at the dirt clinging to my apron and trousers.

"Go," I said to Loomis, who did his best to wipe the smudges off his apron before loping off.

I rounded up as many men as possible and sent them off. I paused long enough to check my hands before making my way to the front of the house. I turned the corner in time to see a sleek carriage in a garish shade of crimson pull up to the front entrance before I fell into place beside Gregor. Footmen stepped forward to open the carriage door and help the occupants out. The first to hit the ground was a short, elderly gentleman with white hair and a polite, if somewhat haughty, expression. The Earl of Candrich acknowledged Lord Bromhurst with a slight bow. The next two men to step out of the carriage couldn't have been more different from the first. Dressed in matching chartreuse jackets and mustard waistcoats, the two tall young gentlemen bowed to the company ranged before them. There was something strange about the way they bent forward, as if they were hinged differently from other men. Gangly. That was the word for it. And more like long-legged birds than men. Richly dressed as they were, nothing could disguise the overly long necks and torsos. Or the oversized noses planted on identical long faces. They towered over their father by at least an arm span.

"Bromhurst, may I present my sons, the Viscount Ditherington and the Honorable St. Peter de Mimsey?" The Earl nodded to each of his sons in turn. The two men folded into awkward bows once more. From down the line, Braden caught my eye. The corner of his mouth twitched. I pressed my lips together and looked away.

"If you do anything," Gregor hissed through clenched teeth, "I'll beat you both to within an inch of your lives."

I squared my shoulders and pulled my face into what I hoped was an expression of soberness.

Lord Bromhurst introduced his daughters in turn. Lord Candrich's expression registered slight approval while his sons looked almost giddy at the sight of so many beautiful women. I tried not to imagine those crane-like forms leaping about excitedly. Gregor would murder me if I began snickering.

The formalities were soon completed, and as one the party entered the manor. Ari looped her arm through Candrich's, and the younger gentlemen claimed Brisella and Canela. Lady Canela's barely veiled disgust made me hope that, for his sake, the Honorable St. Peter de Mimsey kept his hands to himself.

When the family and their guests filed indoors, the staff dispersed. I still wasn't sure where Gregor had stationed me for the day, so I stood aside while he spoke with a couple of other gardeners. My attention was snagged by a round form bustling down the steps of the big house. The head housekeeper stormed up to Gregor, her cheeks ablaze.

Gregor nodded in greeting. "Mrs. Jennings."

"We'll need all new flower arrangements, Gregor," she puffed out.

"Were those from this morning unacceptable?"

"His Grace and his sons have demanded a dance for the evening." She let out a heavy breath. "We didn't anticipate anything of the sort and the ballroom is completely undecorated."

Gregor's demeanor was perfectly accommodating, something only his betters were afforded. He offered her a bow. "Consider it done, Mrs. Jennings."

She sagged with relief. "If only everyone were so cooperative. The kitchen staff is in an uproar."

"Is there anything else I can do to help?" Gregor asked.

"Only about a thousand things," her mouth pulled up at one corner. "But the flowers will do for now."

"Don't hesitate to ask if anything else comes up, Mrs. Jennings. My men would be more than happy to be of assistance."

"Thank you, Gregor." She smiled gratefully before bobbing back into the manor.

"Jonas, take Luke and Aaron with you and gather as many flowers as you can without making anything look too sparse."

Without another word, the three of us headed off in the direction of the shed.

Afternoon passed to evening in a flurry of ruffled feathers and hurried preparations. Only the fact that I wasn't trained to help indoors saved me from most of the chaos, but it didn't stop the ladies' maids or kitchen girls from complaining when they happened upon me. Gratitude filled me when the evening's festivities drew everyone else to the dining hall while the groundskeepers were left to their simple dinner fare.

With my stomach full, the fatigues of the day tugged at me as I neared my bedroom. The thought of finishing the last book Gregor had lent me sounded more tempting by the second.

"Jonas," a feminine voice called out, its urgency pushing all thoughts of retiring for the evening from my mind.

"Yes?" I faced a red-cheeked maid with anxious eyes. I tried to remember her name. Annabelle? Abigail?

"One of the ladies is demanding a fresh bouquet for the dance."

I wanted to ask which of the ladies had made the request, but I knew how impertinent that would sound. "Of course," I said, changing course and heading outdoors once more.

After pocketing a set of clippers, I approached the flower garden. The dusky sky offered little light, but I knew the way well. The heady scent of roses hung about me as I clipped stems. Crickets' songs disrupted the stillness of the evening.

With a handful of flowers clutched in my fist, I made my way along the path that passed the manor. I was about to round the corner and head in the direction of the servants' entrance when a figure in a long gown slipped out the front doors and down the steps.

A breeze stirred her gown and teased the curls hanging on her neck.

"Jonas." My name was little more than a whisper.

The door closed behind her, cutting off the noise of chatting guests and skilled musicians. The crickets' chirping filled the stillness once more.

I moved forward with the flowers held out to her.

"I believe these are for you, My Lady."

Ariela received them with a small smile, her lashes brushing her cheeks as she looked down at the bouquet. Her gown hugged her figure and a smile tickled her lips. I forgot how to breathe.

"I needed a reason to escape from that octopus in there." She tipped her head in the direction of the ballroom.

"You mean His Lordship, the Earl of Candrich?" I tried to keep my tone light, but an edge of jealousy bled through. Maybe she hadn't heard it.

"No." A chuckle of laughter rang out, followed just as quickly by a sigh. "That might have been preferable actually. His Lordship was content to stand aside as his heir put his tentacles all over me."

My jaw clenched and my hands curled into fists. No one would notice if I dragged the viscount out of the manor to pound him into the dirt, would they? I imagined the gangly form bleeding on the ground, his green jacket mottled with blood and dirt. It probably wouldn't be as satisfying as I imagined. He was probably a crier.

"Brisella came to my rescue and sent Abigail after you."

I let out a long breath.

She fingered the petal of one of the roses.

"Any reason she sent for *me*?" The question was bold. I had to know the answer.

"I needed a breath of fresh air."

Fatigue drove me to ask, "Couldn't you have just said that?"

One corner of her mouth curved up into a smile. "Maybe it *was* more than that." She stepped close enough that I could feel the fabric of her skirt brush against my legs. She placed a hand on my chest and gazed up at me through long lashes. Silence stretched between us, the many possible meanings of her words—not to mention her actions—taunting me.

"You'll go out later just the same, won't you?" The accusation dropped from my lips, cooling the space between us that had buzzed with warmth a moment ago.

She averted her eyes and offered no reply.

The sound of the doors opening felt louder than it really was.

"My Lady." The maid from before, Abigail, peeped out. "The Master is asking for you."

"It seems I must be going." Ari tucked an errant

curl back into place, the motion jerky. "Well, thank you . . . what was it again?" She glanced at the lady's maid standing in the doorway.

Abigail mouthed my name.

"Ah yes, thank you for the flowers, Jonas."

I watched her go, her gown swishing. The questions in my mind multiplied by the second, tinged by a layer of anger that hadn't been there before. If Ari refused to address them, I would have to find the answers myself.

಄ಞ

Gregor had fallen asleep long ago. Murmurs from the other servants settling into their own rooms, which had continued until a quarter of an hour ago, didn't bother him in the least. And it was lucky it didn't. He'd have my head if he knew what I planned to do.

A hush fell over the servants' wing, making the occasional snore and rustle of bedclothes from Gregor sound loud. I eased out of my bunk, slipped on my boots, and reached for the dark jacket slung over the footboard. After one last look at Gregor's sleeping form, I pushed the door open and crept down the corridor.

Halfway down the hall, a floorboard creaked behind me. A backward glance revealed no one. With more caution than before, I proceeded outdoors.

The cool air struck me full in the face, raising the hair on the back of my neck. With a bracing breath, I tugged the jacket more tightly around me and made my way around the servants' wing to the rear of the manor.

Shortly, I reached the family's suite of rooms. After the late night of merriment, the lights had been extinguished in every room except for a few on the uppermost floor. The ladies' quarters. From the ground, little could be seen beyond the occasional shadow passing the bank of windows. I would have to find a better vantage point.

I spied a tree with branches about the height of the ladies' rooms. Well-schooled in the rules of the household, I automatically flicked through the consequences of being caught peeping into their chambers: immediate dismissal, a tongue-lashing from Gregor, and possible dismemberment and burning at the stake.

Nothing to be too concerned about.

I shoved my misgivings to the back of my mind, climbed up the trunk, and settled myself amongst the branches. One hand gripped the trunk for safety. A chill breeze ruffled the leaves and tugged at my clothing. I paid it no heed.

Slim forms crossed in front of the closed windows, garbed not in nightclothes but in brightly-colored evening gowns like those they had worn earlier. They straightened hems, tied sashes, and pinned hair into place in a well-practiced manner. The general air of excitement was palpable even from the other side of the glass. After a moment, the ladies threw on wraps and moved out of view. I leaned forward to see where they were going. The branch beneath me creaked ominously with the movement.

A voice sounded below me, "What do you think you're doing?"

The question startled me so badly that my grip on the trunk faltered. The limb beneath me groaned and dipped, and before I could lay hold of the trunk again, the branch gave way and sent me hurtling toward the ground.

I landed flat on my back, pain radiating along my spine and neck. A low groan passed my lips. Above me, the dark sky stretched unforgivingly and the pinprick stars winked in amusement.

They weren't the only ones who were amused.

"If you could have seen yourself," Braden said between snorts of laughter. "One moment you're leering like some good-for-nothing, and the next you're falling from that tree with the most astonished look on your face." He imitated the expression with his mouth hanging open. His face scrunched back up and more snorts interspersed with chortles followed.

Of all the damned misfortunes, I thought, pressing my eyes shut and wishing Braden would leave me to nurse my wounds—both physical and mental—in peace.

After a moment, the snorting ceased and footsteps shuffled nearer. I could feel him peering down at me. The toe of a boot bumped against my ribs. I held in a second moan.

"I should be lecturing you on propriety and the importance of defending a lady's honor rather than putting it in jeopardy. If you'd been caught . . ." I sensed another sermon coming. My head swam at the idea of submitting to further chastisement on respecting my betters. What gave him the right to lecture a wounded man? Especially when he had played a part in the wounding.

"Wait, you're not actually dead, are you?" The question surprised me. After our conversation earlier, I didn't expect compassion. Even then I had no urge to answer. What would he do if I didn't respond?

He applied the boot to my side again, answering the question for me. I raised a hand to push his toe away. "Leave me alone, Braden."

He let out a breath with a whoosh. "It's a relief to know you're alive."

At some point I would probably see the humor of the situation. With most of my body aching from the impact with the ground and with the person who had caused my distress standing by and probably dreaming up some sort of sermon on how nobility should be revered, I currently found it humiliating.

"Come on," Braden urged, thrusting an arm behind my back, "up you go." I preferred to remain on the ground where gravity could do no more damage. Given his nature, Braden wouldn't leave me alone until I showed proper signs of life, so I allowed him to help me up. Another groan escaped as he hauled me up to a sitting position and my head began to swim.

"Now, how do you feel?" This level of solicitousness from Braden was unprecedented. I cracked open my eyes to be sure it was him.

The earnestness on his face was overwhelming. I wanted nothing more than to sink into a hole. Instead, I grunted out, "I'll survive."

"What were you doing up there anyway?" he asked, squinting up at the tree with the newly scarred trunk.

Knowing he wouldn't stop asking until I offered some sort of explanation, I replied, "Just some late night bird watching."

He scoffed. "Awfully big birds."

I couldn't help but chuckle. Pain shot through my chest. I winced and finally gave in. "If you must know, I'm trying to find out what the ladies are doing every night."

"You're worried about them?"

Something in his tone caused me to refocus on his face. All the joviality had drained from his expression.

"Yes," I admitted.

"I only hope something can be done before it's too late."

I raised my eyebrows, willing him to finish the thought.

"You know, before their reputations are irreparably damaged and Lord Bromhurst washes his hands of them."

I nodded. The same thought—coupled with my desire to help Ariela—had spurred my actions. Cocking my head to the side, I screwed up my mouth and squinted at Braden. "What were *you* doing out at this hour?"

He didn't even hesitate. "Following you."

I rolled my eyes. Even that hurt.

"Everyone's noticed your strange behavior. You're lucky Gregor lets you out of his sight. After your appearance in the kitchen gardens, I guessed your odd behavior had to do with the Master's daughters. So, I've been keeping an eye on you."

I recalled the creak I had heard in the hallway. Obviously it had been Braden.

"What do we do now?"

I grimaced. If I hadn't been interrupted while watching the ladies, I might have an answer. As things stood, I had no more to go on than before. I mirrored his shrug. Carefully. "They've already gone wherever it is they were headed."

"You didn't happen to see where they went, did you?" He turned his gaze back to the bank of windows, which were now dark, and peered at them shrewdly. Shrewdness looked foreign on his young face. Trying to make sense of it made my head hurt more than it already did.

"No matter." He focused his attention back to me. "Do you think you can get up? We should probably get you back to bed before anyone is the wiser."

With a heave, he hoisted me to my feet and flung an arm around my waist. I put an arm around his shoulders and did my best not to topple over.

"Here's what I'm thinking," he began, once the tortuous trip to the servants' quarters was underway. "One of the ladies' maids is sweet on me," he said with a smirk. "Perhaps Abigail can be persuaded to help me enter the ladies' chambers."

Unconvinced of his prowess with either subterfuge or the fairer sex, I asked, "And why would she do that?"

"Because silly girls will do anything for the men they're interested in."

I squeezed my eyes shut and refrained from shaking my head. It was bad enough holding in the complaints as every step jarred my aching frame. I wasn't equipped to deal with his ego too.

"Just leave it to me."

I wanted to roll my eyes, but it wasn't worth the pain. "Do as you like, only be careful not to alert anyone to what you're doing —the other maids, the household staff, or any of the family." I tried to convey what I refused to put into words: Ariela and her sisters were in enough trouble without his bumbling attempts at espionage.

"You can trust me," he declared with a broad smile. Maybe it was the fact that every part of me was grumbling in pain, but somehow, that grin didn't make me feel better.

Estella

I awoke to aching muscles and the sun glaring through my window. *Oh no*, I groaned inwardly, *Gregor will have my hide for this.* I struggled to heave myself out of bed, but a meaty palm pushed me back down.

"Oh no, you don't."

I blinked up at Gregor, his square form silhouetted against the window.

"Braden told me what happened." He leaned back in the chair he'd set beside my bed. His bulky frame blocked the light and made it easier to see.

My breath hitched in my chest. "He . . . he did?"

"Yes. I'm surprised you didn't break your neck falling down those stairs." His face fell into the familiar lines of a scowl.

I tried to offer up a smile. Even the attempt hurt.

"You're just lucky Braden heard you. I'd have left you there all night."

A chuckle escaped my mouth. *Ouch.* I pressed a hand to my ribs, silently thanked Braden for his quick thinking, and sank more deeply into my pillow.

"What were you doing up in the middle of the night, anyway?"

With his keen eyes on me, I faltered for a moment before an idea presented itself. "I thought I heard someone sneaking about and went to investigate," I explained, remembering Braden's footstep.

His eyebrows raised, then he nodded as if it all made sense. "It was probably Braden doing the same thing. I can't believe I slept through all of it."

I held in another chuckle—my ribs couldn't take it. One side of my mouth tilted up instead. At least that was bearable.

"Well," he said, pushing himself off the chair, "I must attend to my duties, but you're to remain here for the day. I'll have one of the kitchen girls bring you something to eat. In the meantime, I expect you to rest up. I can't afford to lose you for more than a day, Jonas."

"Thank you, Gregor," I said, receiving no more recognition than a slight bob of the head as he passed though the doorway. I released a sigh of relief. A grudging sense of appreciation for Braden grew within me. Maybe he wasn't completely useless after all.

ཨ☉ॐ

The day lengthened out, punctuated by the visitations of scullery maids bearing food or gossip and of gardeners sneaking in to ask about my health. Between times, I catnapped my way through the morning, doing my best to dwell on neither Ari's predicament nor Braden's sure-to-be-foiled plans to investigate the ladies' chambers. In the life of a servant, a day of liberty was precious and I preferred not to squander it in needless worrying.

"You're looking better than I expected, Jonas," the kitchen girl said when she delivered my midday meal.

Gretchen had always been friendly to me. With her kind nature and lovely face, she represented the type of woman with whom I should be fostering a relationship. However, with Ari holding such a large place in my life, I couldn't think of any other women in that way.

"I still feel horrible."

"Have you heard the news? Maybe that will make you feel better." Gretchen's eyes twinkled with mischief as she placed the plate on my lap.

I brightened, hoping for something good. "No. I've been cooped up all day. I haven't heard anything."

"Then you don't know that the Earl of Candrich and his sons have already departed?"

I shook my head, wondering what Ari and her sisters had done this time.

"The young gentlemen were in the same state as Lord Mansbury when he left. They say the Earl was highly offended." She picked at a string on my blanket. I could tell that if I waited, she would elaborate. "He blames the household for the inebriated behavior of his sons."

"What did Lord Bromhurst have to say about that?" I worried that the ladies' scheming had been revealed at last. The situations were much too identical. Anyone would be suspicious, and rightly so.

"The Master credited their drunkenness to the Earl's overindulgence and their own stupidity," she replied matter-of-factly.

"He doesn't seem to have a high opinion of the Earl or his sons," I ventured.

She shook her head.

"It's refreshing to know that he wouldn't let just anyone marry one of his daughters, even a titled anyone."

Gretchen narrowed her eyes and studied me.

I cleared my throat. "Not yet, anyway."

"No," she agreed, "but it could be that he's holding out for a better title." She searched my face for a moment longer. "Well, I'm due back at my post. If Cook allows it, I'll bring your dinner later."

"Thank you, Gretchen," I said, as she slipped out the door.

Now that I was left on my own again, little distracted me from worrying over what might happen to Ari and her sisters. Had someone discovered what they had done? What if Braden had been found in their rooms? I wanted to be of help, but even sitting up in my bunk hurt. Moving around the room was unimaginable. Confined to my quarters, thoughts of what I might have done if I hadn't been injured and how Braden might bungle things in my absence pestered me. The time passed tortuously slowly while I considered how he could ultimately make everything worse for everyone involved.

At last, the afternoon light faded from the window. My stomach grumbled, informing me that the time for the evening meal had passed. After spending the majority of the afternoon stewing about the precarious situation facing us, I hoped Gretchen would arrive soon to distract me. When the door finally opened, the figure entering was not feminine in the least.

"You look horrible," Braden said, shutting the door and treating me to his widest smile. "Doesn't unemployment agree with you?"

"Where's Gretchen?" I asked, ignoring him. "She promised to bring my supper."

"What, am I not pretty enough for you?" Braden batted his lashes and pursed his lips as he plunked himself in the chair beside my bed.

I refrained from rolling my eyes again. "Gretchen?"

"You're no fun. I was planning to tell you about my discoveries and all you can think about is a measly scullery maid."

I wanted to hear about those discoveries. I needed to hear about them. But I wasn't about to let him know it.

"Fine," he said, "I'll go get your precious Gretchen." He rose from the chair.

I would have preferred to watch him leave. After all, he was the reason I was laid up in bed in the first place. "Wait."

His mouth twisted up into a self-satisfied smirk.

I held in a sigh of forbearance and begged whatever gods may be for patience. "Tell me what happened." I swallowed. "Please."

No more invitation was required. In a second, he reseated himself and poured out the story. "It took very little persuading to enlist Abigail's help. She was more than willing to lend me the key to the ladies' rooms and stand guard while I made a quick inspection." The smugness in his tone made me want to smack him around a little. That, or throw up. Probably the one would follow the other if I attempted it.

"There was nothing," he carried on, oblivious to my inner workings. "I looked through each of their rooms and through the common room as well." He spread his hands in front of him. "Nothing."

I propped myself up on my elbows and tried not to wince at the pain shooting through my chest. "Nothing?" He shook his head. "One moment, a dozen girls are there, and the next they're gone. You saw it yourself, Braden. There must be some explanation." I could hear the frustration seeping into my words.

"Well, there was . . ."

"What?" I demanded. Did he actually know something he wasn't sharing?

His eyes downcast, a blush tinged his cheeks. "Just a . . . a note."

A note? Could it contain a clue to the sisters' plans? Or the name of a possible accomplice?

The blush in his cheeks deepened. "It was in Lari's room."

My brow furrowed. "What did it say?"

"I shouldn't have mentioned it." He continued to avert his eyes. "It's probably nothing."

I channeled all the authoritativeness of the eldest brother of six into my voice. "What did it say?"

"I found it tucked in her diary." He looked down at his hands.

Impatience pushed the question out. "Did it tell anything about what's been going on or where they've been going?"

He offered up a quiet, "No."

"Then why mention it?"

He hesitated before answering. "It was only . . ."

My mind completed the sentence, filling the blank with any number of ridiculous things. Elaborate escape plans, illicit love notes . . .

He put his head in his hands, his voice coming out in a mumble, "It was a note I sent her."

"Of all the . . ." I dropped back onto my pillow. Carefully. "You got me all worked up for nothing?"

His hands fell away from his face. "She kept it!" he retorted. "Doesn't that mean that she considers me a worthy suitor?"

"Worthy suitor?" I scoffed. "It means she has proof of your inappropriate feelings and could easily get you sacked. I'm surprised she hasn't done so already." I shook my head in disgust. "This was a complete waste of time!"

"Fine," he relented, spreading his hands before him. "I looked everywhere, Jonas. There's nothing out of the ordinary."

"I can tell you were very thorough. Did you paw through the ladies' delicates as well?" We were no closer to discovering the truth than before, and my level of annoyance with him had increased. We sat for a moment, my disgust and his embarrassment filling the silence.

"Obviously, there's something odd in that room." I mused, quelling my irritation and picturing the scene as it had been the night before, with all the ladies moving away from the windows. "What about the northwest corner of their sitting room?"

"Northwest?"

"That's where they were headed when you knocked me out of the tree."

"It's not as if I threw a rock at you." He crossed his arms over his chest and scowled. "And you're mentioning this now instead of last night?"

"If you will recall, I had fallen out of a tree. Obviously, I wasn't thinking clearly."

The scowl cleared from his face, replaced by chagrin.

I pressed my eyes closed. I still felt rotten, but that was no reason to be unkind. "So, did you find anything of interest in the northwest corner?"

He shook his head.

"Do you think we could get back in there?" I asked. At the *we* he perked up again.

"Easily."

"Good." My lips curved into a grin as a plan

unfolded in my mind.

೮೦೦೩

A furtive knock sounded at the door.

"One minute," I called out, bracing myself to bend over and pull on my boots. The motion tugged at the bruised muscles across my back and neck. I straightened slowly, hoping it would be the only pain I would suffer that night. When I stepped into the hallway, Braden met me with the widest grin imaginable stretching from one ear to the other. That expression alone made me wary of further damage he might inflict.

"Ready to go?" Braden spoke in a low tone but bounced on the balls of his feet. "The ladies are at dinner, but who knows when one might return for a shawl or something. Time is of the essence!" He uttered the last phrase as if he'd been practicing it for hours, which he probably had.

My head throbbed with pain, which increased with his level of enthusiasm. I looked past Braden. Pressed against the wall was a much more subdued individual in a black dress and apron.

"Abigail?" She glanced up at me, then back down at her feet. "Thank you for what you've done. You've risked a great deal to help us." Her cheeks pinked and she looked up again, this time holding my gaze.

Braden popped between us. "Oh, she doesn't mind." He beamed at her and she smiled shyly back. He turned back to me. "Now, can we go?"

I didn't want to feed his enthusiasm by agreeing, but waiting longer increased the danger of being caught. I waved him onward.

Braden grabbed Abigail by the hand and towed her down the hall. I followed in their wake, a headache throbbing at the back of my skull.

A trip up the back stairs and down various corridors—some of which required stealth to avoid attracting notice—brought us to the ladies' suite of rooms. Abigail unlocked the door and slipped inside. Braden had arranged for her to clear the rooms before we entered. A moment later, she emerged. She held the door open and motioned for us to enter.

Braden followed me, pausing on the threshold to talk to Abigail. I half-expected him to give her a ridiculous code word to call out if someone came by. It would be just like him to make the process more dramatic than necessary. He surprised me by only asking her to stand guard and intercept anyone who tried to enter. When she agreed, he eased the door shut. The rooms fell into the dimness of early evening, relieved only by a few flickering lamps. Branching off the main sitting room were several doors leading to individual bedchambers. I recalled the events of the night before, remembering the sisters gathering in the main room before disappearing. Losing no time, I made my way behind shadowy settees, curved armchairs, and spindle-legged tables covered with lamps and the type of breakable items women seemed to favor, to the northwest corner. I inched between a bulky armchair and a floor lamp with a cut-glass shade, and slid into the corner opposite the window I'd been spying through the night before. A shelf littered with books, ceramics, and a large vase occupied the adjoining wall. I was about to reach around it to run my fingers over the wall when the vase began to totter. I thrust out a hand to steady it at the same time Braden's shot out and toppled it in the opposite direction.

"Whoops!" he uttered as the vase and a couple of other items careened toward the floor. He lunged for the vase while I made a grab for everything else, my back wrenching in the process.

He snatched the vase out of the air right before impact.

With the other things clutched safely in my hands, I glared at him and tried to breathe shallowly to calm the pain in my back.

"Sorry!"

I continued to scowl. He'd been unnaturally quiet before he'd bumbled into the shelf. I wanted to demand what he'd been thinking. But why bother? There was no cure for stupidity.

I motioned for him to step back. He moved only a few inches. I raised my eyebrows, intensifying the dull throb at the back of my head. It was worth the pain. Finally, Braden took the clue and edged further away. Only when he stood at a safe distance did I examine the porcelain figurines cupped in my hands. I turned the lamp up and held them under the light to be sure they weren't damaged. Figurines of two young girls with light hair and pastel skirts streaming behind them as if stirred by the wind. The resemblance to Ari's younger twin sisters, Estella and Frizella, was unmistakable. The twins had the same adventurous spirit that had been captured in the figurines. Looking at them brought something to mind that I'd nearly forgotten.

I placed the porcelain figures back on the shelf, turned back to the place where the two walls met, and ran my fingers over it.

"What is it?" Braden asked, from just over my shoulder.

I shot him a warning look. He stepped back, but the expectant look in his eyes urged me to answer before he did something stupid. Something else stupid.

"The twins," I said finally, turning to address him.

"What about them?"

"When the family moved into the manor from their previous home—"

"They didn't always live here?" Braden interrupted.

I shook my head. "This was Lord Bromhurst's childhood home. He and the family only moved in after his father's death when he inherited the title and the lands."

Braden nodded in understanding.

"Estella and Frizella, who were about nine-years-old at the time, were obsessed with trapdoors and secret passageways. They searched everywhere."

"And?" he prompted.

I turned back to the wall to continue my investigation. "As far as I know, they never found anything."

He scoffed.

"But what if they *did* find something? This house is riddled with—" Something beneath my palms caused me to pause. Cool air flowed over my fingertips. I ran them up and down in the same area and felt the same coolness. I moved more slowly, and detected a slight indentation. I pressed it firmly and a loud click sounded. "This house is riddled with unused space," I finished, "almost as if the inside doesn't fit the outside."

Braden was back at my shoulder. Even he was rendered mute when the section of wall swung noiselessly outward. Cool air rushed forth, enveloping both of us as the door opened onto darkness. The shelf still stood in the way. A slight amount of pressure slid it aside without causing any of the items it contained to even wobble. The doorway gaped open before me, taunting me with the mystery of what lay beyond. Could it be the land of mystery where the ladies spent their evenings? An underground kingdom of gold and silver where every freedom awaited? Braden's rapid breathing at my side told me he too was eager to discover where the passage led. At that moment, a knock sounded at the door, freezing me in place.

Braden muttered something uncomplimentary about Abigail and nearly knocked me over in his haste to reach the door. I reeled before regaining my balance, pain from the sudden movement shooting down my spine as I fumbled to close the secret door and slide the shelf into place. I braced myself against the wall until the pain subsided. Then, I followed Braden to the doorway where he whispered furtively with Abigail.

"She was about to enter when I headed her off," Abigail explained. "I've a feeling they'll be finishing soon and then who knows what might happen. I must take Lady Larela's wrap down or they'll send another maid after it."

"Of course, Abigail." I waved her into the main room even though I couldn't think of anything but the hidden space we'd discovered. "You can't keep Lady Larela waiting. We've finished here anyway."

The tilt of Braden's eyebrows questioned my decision. He wanted to explore as badly as I.

In the hallway once more, we watched Abigail hurry off with Larela's wrap before we turned towards the servant's wing.

"That was enlightening," Braden declared. "Who would have guessed—"

I cocked my head and gave him a warning look. "Not a word." His disappointment pulled the corners of his mouth down. "Not to Abigail or to anyone else you're trying to impress. If we want to be of any help, we can't tell anyone what we've found."

He nodded in response, his head bobbing.

"Now, if you care to discuss this in private, I'll be in my room."

"I can bring you a dinner tray," he replied without prompting, heading toward the kitchens with a spring in his step.

ℰↄ℘

"Where have you been?"

Gregor's words froze me in place, halfway into the bedchamber we shared.

"Well?"

"The facilities," I muttered, saying the first thing that came to mind. "I visited the facilities."

His eyebrows rose. "For over half an hour?"

"Uh . . ." How long had he been waiting? Every excuse that explained a prolonged trip to the necessary sounded worse than the last. I chose the most innocent. "My stomach has been touchy since last night."

His face pulled into an expression of disgust.

No matter what he was thinking, it was benign compared to setting foot in the ladies' rooms. If he discovered what I had really been up to, I would be out of a job quicker than you could say *secret passageway.*

His eyes narrowed. "Regardless of what you've really been doing, you're expected back at your post in the morning."

"Of course, Gregor."

"I trust your stomach issues will be resolved by then?"

"I'm sure they will."

"Good. I have other things to see to." He pushed past me into the hallway.

I let out a breath. Whether Gregor believed me or not, one thing was certain, he would ensure that I was back at work and up to no mischief in the morning. I sat down on my bed and stared at the door.

After avoiding a serious reprimand from Gregor, I couldn't be caught out of my room again. Even if I did need to use the necessary. I had no choice but to wait for Braden to return.

He's probably flirting with the housemaids, I thought. His inability to focus on anything other than women, or on making my life a living hell, bothered me more than I cared to admit. Especially when Gregor could return at any moment. It was just as well. Exploring the hidden passageway would satisfy my curiosity about where the sisters went each night, but only following the sisters when they went would reveal what they did there.

At last, the door swung open. Without knocking or asking for permission, Braden walked in. Since he bore a tray laden with stew, crusty rolls, fresh butter, and mugs of frothy cider, I wouldn't complain. About that anyway.

"It's about time," I said, eyeing the food he parceled out between two plates. The smell of fresh bread fostered a wave of hunger pangs.

"Sorry," Braden said automatically. "I had to explain my absence to the other gardeners and make sure Abigail hadn't gotten into trouble either."

"I trust everything is all right?" I'd been too preoccupied to think of Abigail or all she had done to help us.

"No one suspects a thing."

I found his calmness reassuring and made a mental

note to be kinder to him. It wasn't his fault that he swung between being overbearing and being obnoxious. Maybe no one had ever taught him how to interact appropriately with his peers.

When we were both settled with plates of food in our laps, he jumped right to the problem at hand.

"So, what's the plan?"

I popped half of a buttered roll in my mouth and began to chew before answering. "The ladies always meet in the sitting room in the evening to spend time with their father and practice their music and stitching. If we sneak into their chambers then and wait until everyone retires—"

"We can follow them!" he finished, waving his spoon in the air for emphasis. A blob of gravy hit me in the face.

"Exactly." I wiped my cheek with my sleeve.

"Sorry." Braden grimaced. "I'll ask Abigail if she doesn't mind telling us when they're out of the way tonight," Braden said around a mouthful of stew.

"I don't want to put her in any more danger."

"It's fine," he replied, dismissively. "She doesn't even have to stay behind this time. As long as she makes sure no one is about, we can sneak right in."

I wanted to be sure he understood the gravity of the proposal. "This isn't a game, Braden. If Gregor hears anything about it, we'll lose our positions. And if anyone finds out Abigail has helped us, she will too. What we're doing is strictly forbidden."

"I know." His brow furrowed. "But the ladies need

our help. I can't see any other way forward."

I found myself nodding.

"Then it's settled: tonight is the night!" He raised his mug, sending the cider rushing over the lip.

I raised my mug and carefully clinked it with his. "Tonight."

ജ⊃ര

The brown jacket draped over my arm felt conspicuous considering that we weren't venturing outside. Dressing in dark clothing while I sneaked around outdoors had been one thing, wearing it indoors felt ridiculous. I had agreed with Braden's suggestion only to get him to shut up. Now the thought of putting it on and lying in wait for the ladies to return to their rooms seemed more like something a highwayman might do. Heroes didn't make a point of lurking in dark passageways waiting for unsuspecting maidens.

Braden's loud knock sounded at the door. I braced myself for the worst, but hoped for the best, and pulled it open.

Dressed in head-to-toe black, including a well-tailored riding coat, he greeted me with an enormous grin.

I couldn't stop the reproach from tumbling out of my mouth. "Where did you get that coat? The Master's closet? In that get-up everyone will assume you're out to rob the rich to give to the poor. All that's missing is a mask."

He chuckled, eying my clothing with amusement.

He didn't have to tell me his thoughts. I wore dark clothing as well, but only brown trousers, a shirt, and my regular work boots. The coat still hung on my arm.

Uninterested in what he had to say, I stepped around him and trudged down the hallway. We had planned to leave the servant's quarters while everyone was gathered in the dining hall. I prayed that the few people lingering in the hallways would attribute the sight of two men dressed as we were to one of Braden's larks.

"We may as well get this over with. Have the women left their rooms?"

"Absolutely. Abigail promised to leave the door unlocked for us. And Gregor is taken care of as well."

That was the trickiest part of the plan. Gregor, who had already become suspicious, had to be kept occupied. No one would raise the alarm quicker than he if I were found out of bed again.

"Loomis agreed?" To hang the plan on the shoulders of a confirmed idiot was foolish at best. But Braden was already involved. What further damage could Loomis do?

"I gave him all my pocket money and instructed him to keep Gregor at the card tables in town well into the night."

"Do you think he's capable of that?" I pictured Loomis taking said pocket money and treating himself to a night of food, drink, and wenches at the local tavern. However, if there was a woman who could be bought by the likes of Loomis, or enough liquor to bring about such an event, I had yet to hear of it. Even wenches had their standards.

"We discussed it very carefully," Braden assured me.

"Multiple times?" Loomis still couldn't remember which end of the hoe was used for hoeing.

"Of course," Braden assured me. "I repeated it until he could repeat it back to me. Abigail sent a message to her friend who works in the public house. She's been instructed to keep an eye on the two, as well as make sure Gregor's mug is full all night."

I nodded, feeling impressed.

"What do you think we'll find in that passageway?" Braden asked.

"I have no idea. Answers, I hope."

At last we reached the ladies' quarters, and after ensuring that no one was watching, I eased the door open and stepped inside. The main room was brighter than it had been before, alight with the glow of a fire in the hearth and various lamps scattered around the room. As I had done earlier, I made my way past the many pieces of furniture to the bookcase with the twin figurines atop it. I heard the door shut and Braden's muffled tread as he crossed the carpeted floor.

"Careful," I warned. "We can't afford any more mishaps."

"Yes, My Lord," he replied.

I rolled my eyes. Turning back to the corner, I searched for the latch that released the hidden door. Even with the added light, it was impossible to make out. I ran my fingertips over the wall as I had done before and located it quickly. A click sounded and the door swung inward.

The scent of unused rooms and a faint dankness like that of the underground met me. Braden bumped into me to get a better look and almost knocked me down the set of stairs that began less than a pace away.

"Oops!" he said, steadying me. "Careful!"

I wanted to retort that if anything were to happen, he would be the cause. I kept my thoughts to myself, for at that moment I heard the creak of the outer door accompanied by the unmistakable chatter of females. I wasted no time in sliding the bookcase aside to access the passageway.

"Quickly!" I said in a harsh whisper, grabbing his cloak and yanking him toward the opening.

"But, where do you suppose it leads?"

"I have no idea, but it's better than being caught in here!" I gave him another shove and stepped down into the darkness before sliding the bookcase into place and swinging the door closed. Once the door had shut, a wide strip of light at the bottom bled into the darkness. Braden began to speak, and I clapped a hand over his mouth. From the sound filtering through the hidden door, the ladies had entered the sitting room. Hopefully they noticed nothing out of the ordinary. Braden's face was barely discernible in the dim light, but I treated him to one of my sternest looks anyway and motioned for him to stay quiet. When I felt his head nod in response, I took my hand off his mouth. We crouched down. I wrapped a hand around my chest as my ribs and back complained about the movement. I pressed my ear to the panel to hear better.

"I can't take one more minute of Gissela's playing," a youthful female voice declared.

"And it seems as if Hayla's actually becoming worse," a similar voice added.

"And don't even talk to me about Issela," they said as one.

Their declarations were met with bell-like laughter.

"Really, you two are terrible." The soft tone could belong only to Lady Brisella, and the other two must be—

"You have to admit," began one.

"Silence is preferable," finished the other.

It had to be the identical twins, Lady Estella and Lady Frizella. They possessed a truly unique way of conversing, often finishing one another's sentences as if they were thinking the same thing. Even after several years in their father's employ, I could not tell them apart. Their sisters, however, seemed to have no such difficulty.

Brisella's laughter rang out once more. "Then it's fortunate you both came down with headaches and requested my assistance."

"No one else would do," said Estella or Frizella.

"True," continued Frizella or Estella. "Only you have ever been effective at curing a headache, dearest Bree."

"Yes," added the first. "The rest only know how to cause them." They both giggled, their laughter so similar it sounded like its own echo.

"Perhaps you should both lie down," Brisella commented, "in case someone comes in."

"All right," Estella and Frizella chorused.

"As long as we don't have to be quiet, Bree," one of them said.

"Because we'd like to talk about last night!"

I looked at Braden and raised my eyebrows, only to find his eyes wide enough that I could see the glimmer of the whites in the dark. In his haste to press his ear even tighter to the door, he lost his footing on the step and nearly tumbled backwards down the staircase. I caught at the front of his shirt just in time to yank him back up. We had barely avoided disaster, but nothing could mask the scuffling his feet had made. My back and chest ached from the strain of holding him. My pulse thudded in my ears and Braden's rapid breath was so loud that surely they would hear it too. We froze, unable to do more than listen for the sisters' reactions.

"What was that?" the twins asked in unison.

Brisella's voice was calm when she replied, "Probably just a rat." I blew out my breath.

"A rat?!" her sisters yelled. I could practically see them falling over one another to get their feet off the floor.

"Oh," Brisella scoffed, "there's no need to carry on so. You know the manor is full of them. And if you two weren't allergic, we could keep a cat to take care of them. Krisela would love that."

"Cats!" exclaimed one sister.

"Nearly as filthy as rats!" added the other. "I don't see how Kris can tolerate them."

"Cats are lovely," Brisella said. "All silky fur and independence. Like Ari."

The girls tittered.

"And you know who's exactly like a dog?" Either Frizella or Estella asked.

"All floppy hair and loyalty?" the other added.

They burst into giggles again, but between the laughter I caught my name. My ears burned.

"You know he would do anything for Ariela. If I had that kind of power . . ." one of the twins said. The end of the sentence was lost in the giggles that followed.

"For one thing, he'd always be bringing *me* fresh flowers," her sister finished.

"And meeting *me* in secluded locations," the other added.

I squeezed my eyes shut in an attempt to block out the rest of the conversation. I had no idea how they'd learned about my interactions with Ari. What would happen if they revealed it to their father? Losing my position would be the least of my worries.

The adage had proven true. Those who listened at keyholes—or hidden doors, as the case may be—heard nothing good about themselves.

"He's nothing like the young gardener who has his eye on Lari."

"Oh, yes," said her twin, "the young one is ever so handsome."

Braden elbowed me in the ribs, almost knocking me off the top step in the process. *Ouch.* I rubbed my side and glowered at him even though he couldn't read my expression in the dim light. A lift to his ears, however, led me to believe his grin stretched from ear to ear. The urge to shove him down the stairs possessed me. But not only would the effort hurt me physically, it would also alert the sisters to our presence. I pushed the notion aside and turned my attention back to the party conversing on the other side of the wall.

"Don't the two of you have someone else in mind?"

"Oh, yes," they replied, sighing with pleasure. "Who could look at anyone else?"

Brisella let out a low chuckle. "I thought you two were smitten. You're nearly as bad as that young gardener mooning over Lari."

I wasn't the only one who knew of Braden's affection for Lady Larela. I wondered how many others had noticed. I had been careful to conceal my feelings for Ari, but if they knew about that, what else did they know?

"I know Ari wants us to put an end to our getaways, but how can we be expected to return to normal life after six months of bliss?"

Six months?

"The life Father would have us lead is so boring," one of the twins exclaimed, carrying on where her sister had left off. "Music, needlework, polite conversation . . ."

"We just want to live like regular people. Is that so

impossible?"

Still reeling from the fact that they had been escaping right out from under their father's nose for half a year, I barely noticed that their older sister had made no reply. Brisella was usually firmly in Ari's camp, but I had no clue how she might respond. Had she been won over by the temptation of liberty?

"And what if Father has his way? What if all of this leads to a life of even more bondage?"

Stunned silence met Lady Brisella's words.

After a moment, she added, "In homes of our own with husbands to please and households to run, we'll hardly ever see one another."

"We couldn't be separated!" the young girls replied together, probably clutching at one another as if at any moment a nobleman would arrive to drag one of them off by the hair.

Brisella's voice cut through the pandemonium. "Then we must listen to Ari. We have to be prepared to return to normal life."

"Surely Father can be made to see sense," one twin declared.

"And then there will be no need to abandon our nightly ventures," the other added.

A sigh sounded, deep and long. "You know that won't happen. He would never approve of what we've been doing. The only thing to do now is to make sure as little damage has been done as possible."

"By putting an end to all of it, you mean?"

"The only pleasure we have in life?"

"Yes," Brisella answered.

"But not yet!" the twins pleaded.

"Where would we wear our prettiest gowns?"

"And find gentlemen so obliging?"

"And handsome?"

The questions tumbled over one another like a waterfall, one beginning where the other left off. I imagined them begging on their knees with their hands clasped. The twins were as fond of dramatics as Braden.

"Very well," Brisella responded. "But soon, my dears."

Tweets, chirps, and shrieks of girlish enthusiasm met this comment. The rest of the conversation was swallowed up in it, the twins talking over one another until nothing was discernible from the other side of the wall. I wanted to talk over this new development with Braden and discover what he made of it, but even the slightest noise might give us away. Or send the young women after a rat catcher.

"Now, ladies," Brisella's voice rang over the hubbub, "I believe it's time to return. The evening is nearly over. By this time, our sisters will have put an end to the musical entertainment."

The other two assented, their footsteps and voices growing fainter as they made their way out of their rooms. Even after the door clicked shut, I couldn't find the words to speak. It was too unbelievable.

Braden however, suffered from no such impediment. When he spoke, his words sounded incredibly loud. "Can you believe they've been at it for half a year?"

I considered for a moment. Had Ari shown signs of being involved for that long? It had been less than a month since she'd come to me and admitted that something was going on. But *six months*? I shook my head in disbelief.

I fumbled to open the door; my palm caught on a handle. In another second light poured into our hiding place. We moved the bookcase aside and swung the door fully open.

"I can't believe it," Braden said quietly, sitting in the doorway, drawing his knees up to his chest, and wrapping his arms around them. "What can be so fascinating that they've willingly gone against their father's orders?"

Having spoken with Ari, I pieced together enough to understand. Twelve children—and especially twelve grown daughters—were difficult to handle. After the death of his wife, Lord Bromhurst's edicts had grown in number and severity. The more he exerted his control, the more determined his daughters became to duck his orders.

"What do you make of it?" Braden asked.

"Which part?"

He shrugged. "All of it."

I looked down at him and considered the conversation. "It's as I feared. Now that her sisters have tasted freedom, they don't want to return to ordinary life."

Braden looked uncomfortable. "And what about . . ."

I raised my eyebrows. Whether he took it as a warning to tread carefully or as encouragement to continue, I couldn't say.

"They compared you to a loyal dog," he finished, as if daring me to be angry.

I grunted, rejoining with, "And apparently you're a lovesick puppy."

Braden chuckled.

"It doesn't matter," I brushed it off with a wave of my hand, even though the thought that so many knew of my interaction with Ari made me anxious. "It sheds little light on the problem at hand." I faced the hidden staircase, looked down it. Little was visible past the few steps on which we stood.

"This might help." Braden stood, entered the room, and returned with a lamp. He tilted it so the light shone down the stairway. Even with the lamplight, little could be discerned.

"I can't see where it leads." Braden craned his head to see further. "Is that a landing further down?"

I squinted into the dimness and made out a wide landing about one floor down, half-covered with bulky objects. "Appears to be."

"It might make a better hiding place than this." If we remained where we were, one wrong movement from the ladies entering the stairwell and not only would our presence be made known, but both of us would also be sent tumbling down the steps.

"If only we could take the light with us," I muttered. Taking the lamp would be unwise, as its absence would warn the ladies that someone had been in their rooms.

With the lamp in one hand, Braden patted down his pockets with the other, like he was looking for loose change. He dug in a pocket, pulled out his fist, and thrust something into my face. With an expression of triumph, he asked, "Will this help?"

I palmed the object, holding it up so I could see it more clearly. A candle stub. "And how do you happen to be carrying this?"

He shrugged again. "Never know when you might need it."

I had nothing quite so useful in my pockets. But my younger brothers, who had often kept their pockets full of string, dead mice, and other oddities, came to mind.

"May I?" Braden put forth his hand to take the candle. Setting the lamp back in the ladies' rooms, he removed its glass shade and touched the stub of wax to the burning wick. After a second, the candle ignited.

"Shall we?" Braden made his way down the stairs with the burning candle held aloft.

I slid the bookcase back and eased the door shut before following.

"Can you see anything?" I asked, my voice hushed. The slight echo of our steps felt louder in the dark.

"Not much."

I looked around at the raw wood walls surrounding us. A narrow, winding back staircase, like the one built for the servants, met my eye. Spider webs strung over beams, corners, and the slim handrail. Only the steps themselves were free of dust.

Braden paused a few paces in front of me. "This is it." He set the candle down on the broad landing and sat beside it.

I peered around him. Crates of various sizes draped in heavy canvas occupied half the landing. From the amount of dust clinging to their trappings, they'd been stored there for some time. Maybe even before the family had taken up residence.

"Do you want to go further?" Braden asked.

I looked down the stairs. The longer we descended, the cooler the air became. The scent tingeing it had also changed from stale to earthy. Our present location afforded only a partial view of what lay below. I looked up and saw the vague outline of the hidden door.

"No. This is as good a place as any to wait. The crates will hide us well and we'll be able to see and hear them coming."

A curious look took over Braden's face, twisting a corner of his mouth down. "What happens if they bring a light, like we did?"

"They'd be fools to attempt the stairs without one, but if we stay out of sight and keep quiet, there's no reason for them to know we're here."

We stepped around the items littering the landing, shifting them and disturbing the dust as little as possible, until we couldn't be seen either from above or from the landing itself. Cramped into a corner, we made ourselves as comfortable as possible. While the candle burned down to nothing, we waited for the girls to come.

Frizella

Cramped into a musty back staircase beside Braden, I should have been able to stay alert, but the trauma of the past few days had taken a toll, and I fell into a fitful slumber. Even the fact that my ribs ached and my legs were pins and needles all over didn't keep the exhaustion at bay. Light flooding the stairwell from above and the hum of chatting voices brought me fully to my senses. That, and Braden's finger jabbing at my side. I winced and shoved his hand away. The voices grew louder, accented by the soft tread of slippers on the steps. Careful to be sure I remained hidden, I watched the light flicker off the walls as the ladies approached.

A familiar voice pulled at me. I couldn't make out the words, but something that sounded like my name floated down to me. After a second, Brisella's hushed words could be heard. "As I understand, he's had some sort of accident."

I caught Ariela's reply. "That must be why I didn't see him today. Do you know if he's all right?"

Braden poked me again. How did he manage to target the sore spot every time? I shoved him away and rubbed at my side. I considered punching him in the stomach for good measure.

"As far as I know, he's taken the day off and the maids are tending to his needs."

"Which maids?" Ari asked brusquely.

"Gretchen and Abigail, I think."

An unladylike scoff emitted from Ari.

"No, no," Brisella reassured her. "Gretchen's no harm and Abigail's smitten with that young gardener, the one obsessed with Larela."

"It's not any of my business whom Abigail makes cow eyes at," Ari replied.

I knew just the expression she meant. Abigail's eyes beamed with adoration whenever Braden happened to be near. I bit my lip to keep from snickering.

"Of course," Brisella replied, nonchalantly, "it's not as if Jonas means anything to you, does he?"

"He's my friend. That's all."

The dismissive tone in her voice cut me to the quick. I reminded myself that even admitting to a friendship was forbidden. Yet, hearing her sum up our relationship in that manner hurt more than my injured ribs, aching back, and cramped legs all put together.

The girls reached our landing and paused. I couldn't help myself. I leaned out around the crates and boxes piled between us far enough to catch a glimpse of Ari, her profile sharp in the light from the lamp she clutched. She faced her sisters. "Is everyone accounted for?"

Larela's soprano called from above, "Everyone's here, Ari. And before you ask, I have the other lamp and I've already secured the door."

"Very well. Take care on the steps, ladies." The sisters murmured assent and once again they began to descend.

With the treading of twelve pairs of feet to cover the sound, Braden whispered in my ear. "When do we follow?"

"In a moment. Be patient."

"What if we lose them?" If he had his way, we'd trail after Larela all night.

"Twelve girls who are not even trying to move quietly?" I whispered back. "We can afford to wait until they've passed. When the light reaches the bottom of the staircase, we'll follow them."

The triplets, Gissela, Issela, and Hayla, passed, deep in an argument. Their voices rang discordantly in the narrow stairwell. If the sisters were lined up by age— the only reason these three would be grouped together—then the parade was nearly at an end. I listened for Larela's voice.

"What do you expect?" Her soprano voice sounded in the stairwell. Braden pushed me out of the way for a glimpse of his ladylove. Hopefully she didn't hear the resulting scuffle as I muffled a groan and pushed Braden back.

"He seems so devoted." Krisela stopped on the landing to wait for her younger sister to catch up.

"Oh yes, *so* devoted," Larela replied bitterly. "Until someone more convenient comes along. If I ever get my hands on that minx Abigail . . ."

Beside me, I could practically feel Braden's smugness. Once again, the urge to toss him down the stairs seized me. But, if ever there were a moment to curb one's baser desires, this was it. Besides, the action would probably hurt me far more than it would hurt him.

The girls rustled past, their conversation growing fainter by the second. By now Larela had reached the bottom. The light in her hand glowed at the base of the stairs. I turned to Braden. "Let's go."

We crept down the staircase, hoping the noise created by the girls would quiet the sounds of our passage. I kept my eyes on the fading light. Wishing neither to take the staircase in complete darkness nor to lose track of the sisters, I maintained a safe distance between us.

The wooden walls housing the stairwell began to feel different. The temperature dropping as we descended made me grateful for the jacket I had brought. The scent tingeing the air became earthier. Just before the light disappeared, we reached the bottom and found a rock tunnel connected to it. From the faint hum of conversation and the light receding along it, the sisters had obviously taken the route through the tunnel.

The last of the light flickered off the walls,

revealing pits in the surface and streams of something trickling down from above. I placed a hand on the wall to get my bearings and was dismayed by the coating of slime covering the rock. I wiped my fingers on my coat and continued with my hands at my side. The underground portion of the passage had shallow, stone-hewn steps. Every once in a while, Braden clutched at my shoulder for support when he hit a slippery spot. I waited until he seemed steadier before proceeding. Up ahead, the ladies' voices were little more than whispers. Larela's light still beamed at the end of the tunnel and marked their steady progress.

At length, a fresher smell entered the passageway. If the hidden stairway led underground, it might let out somewhere in the manor grounds or nearby forest. Situated on a slight rise, the manor and its grounds spread for miles in most directions. By my calculations, the tunnel headed to the east where the forest lay. The flickering light seemed to have stopped a few paces below and was moving away from the tunnel. I breathed more easily. Unfamiliar passageways unsettled me, especially in near darkness.

We followed the sound of the ladies into another corridor, this one slanting upward. Beyond the sounds emitted when he slipped and lost his balance, Braden had not spoken the entire time.

"Are you all right?"

"Fine," he said, his tone higher than usual.

I tossed him a look, but could make out nothing of his expression. "Really?"

"I'm not overly fond of tight places."

"Well, if the fresh air is anything to go by, we should come out somewhere soon."

He grunted his approval and we continued onward.

A faint breeze entering the passageway chased away the last of the staleness. The air freshened with each step and the darkness began to lessen. The tunnel stopped in some type of cavern, the mouth covered with leafy vines. Moonlight crept between the leaves to illuminate the opening. A cacophony of voices could be heard from the other side of the vines: high and low, male and female. We crept to the curtain of greenery. Beside me, Braden peeked through the vines.

"Men? They meet *men* every night?"

I remembered what the twins had said about handsome, obliging gentlemen. My jaw tightened. I pushed the words out from between my clenched teeth. "It would seem so."

Now that the group had assembled, several men could be seen intermingling with the sisters in a small clearing between the cavern and the edge of the forest. From the preening behavior of Canela, Larela, and the twins, these men were both well known and well liked. The lamps the sisters had brought with them were nowhere in sight, but the moonlight was bright enough to illuminate the scene. Without meaning to, I scanned the crowd for Ariela. She stood close to the tree line, side-by-side with Brisella and two men. The man nearest Ari leaned toward her with his head cocked to the side, and his eyes fixed on her.

I hated him on sight.

From this distance and with nothing stronger than moonlight, Ari's opinion of her companion was impossible to gauge. Though she hadn't pushed him away, she wasn't holding his hand or plastered to his side like Canela was with her partner.

After a moment, Ari lifted her chin and her voice rang over the assembly. "The night wanes. Shall we, gentlemen?"

The man at her side offered her his arm. Like the rest in the company, he wore respectable clothing, neither noticeably cheap nor fine like the suits the Master favored. Based on that alone, I supposed the man to be well-born, though probably untitled. One thing was certain; Lord Bromhurst wouldn't deem him worthy of wooing his daughter. No matter how desperate His Lordship became.

In this case, I agreed.

The man's low status didn't bother Ari. Without a second's hesitation, she took his arm and together they led the way through the small clearing and into the woods.

I almost stepped out after the pair, but Braden's firm grip on my arm held me in place. Half of a snarl passed my lips.

"I know how you feel."

My anger was cut short. I followed his gaze and saw Larela in a tête-à-tête with the youngest of the gentlemen. Apparently she had just said something funny, for he threw back his head to laugh and flung an arm around her to squeeze her waist in a familiar way.

From the flaring of his nostrils, I thought Braden might barrel into the clearing and give us away. Instead he closed his eyes and took a deep breath, his grip on my arm becoming almost painfully tight. Releasing both the breath and the death grip on my arm, he said, "It will do no good to chase after them in a jealous fit. If we want to help them, we must remain levelheaded."

Whether he spoke the words for my benefit or his own, he was speaking sense. Maybe our time in the corridor leading from the manor had done permanent damage to his mental faculties. I considered checking him over, but as I was neither his elder brother nor his nursemaid, I did nothing.

"They're headed into the forest anyway. It will be easy enough to track them there," he added.

I turned my attention back to the ladies. Most had disappeared into the trees already. Only a few remained to follow the slim track through the forest. Once again, Larela trailed at the end of the procession.

"Let's give them a head start." I said.

Braden nodded. After a full three minutes, I pushed aside the vines and proceeded into the glade. The moonlight shone down, pooling in the clearing. We kept the trail in sight and passed through the trees instead. Braden padded soundlessly behind while I did my best not to imitate an elephant crashing through the brush.

"How are you doing that?" I tossed over my shoulder in a harsh whisper.

"I spent a lot of time in the forest when I was a boy," he said in a low tone.

"And?" I said, "Every boy does that. Until his mother calls him in for supper."

"Well, yes," Braden admitted. "It was my father who grew uneasy when I disappeared without telling anyone where I was headed. He'd send the men out after me. I didn't like having all my fun ruined, so I learned to sneak around as quietly as the forest animals themselves. It became a sort of game, if you will."

A different picture of his home life snapped into place in my mind. I had assumed that, like me, Braden was born and bred for work. "Why would a man like your father send his son into service?"

His answer was automatic. "He didn't. He died a short time ago."

I cocked an eyebrow. "And the rest of your family?"

"My mother died when I was young. There was no one else."

Fatherless and with no other choice but to go into service. I began to feel sympathetic toward Braden. He couldn't be out of his teen years and had already suffered great loss.

I thought of my large family. Even though I had been out on my own for some time, I knew they stood behind me. The older brother in me wanted to comfort Braden for his losses. I clapped a hand on his shoulder. "I'm sorry."

He turned back. "You couldn't have known." He

119

offered up a crooked grin and added, "And at least you let me tag along. This is the most fun I've had in a long time."

I thought of the way he had practically blackmailed me. "You didn't leave me much of a choice."

He chuckled before resuming the trek through the forest. "I can be persuasive when I want something badly enough."

I wandered in his wake, digesting everything I'd just learned. I never would have imagined that Braden's experiences prior to arriving at the manor had been any different from mine. How would it have been to grow up in something other than poverty, where working to put bread on the table wasn't as familiar as breathing? I could never have run away without worrying whether the family would have enough to eat or if the crops could be gathered before bad weather struck.

It was as difficult to comprehend as a group of young noblewomen sneaking off for midnight trysts with strange men.

Images of Ariela on the other man's arm and the admiration in his eyes replayed in my mind. The familiarity between the two was further proof of the time they had spent together. I set my jaw and quickened my pace.

At length, we heard voices ahead and slowed down. A few of the girls, their dresses bright against the dark trunks and deep green of the forest, meandered along the path with their partners. Braden motioned for me to hurry along. I did as he directed, hoping to catch a bit more of their conversation while they dallied in the woods. In my haste to draw nearer to the group, I forgot to place my feet carefully and a thick twig snapped beneath my heel. Braden looked back with a grimace. Up ahead, the ladies' and gentlemen's conversation paused.

"What was that?" chorused several female voices.

"Quick!" Braden muttered, grabbing my arm and dragging me toward a fallen tree trunk. We crouched behind it and listened for the others' approach.

"It came from over there," a feminine voice exclaimed.

"Probably nothing more than forest animals," one of the men responded.

"What if it's something else . . ." Larela's voice, as clear as a bell, rang out. "What if someone's followed us?"

"That's impossible," a pompous male voice answered. "No one could find that trail without being led to it."

"All the same," Larela's voice took on a sweet quality, the same one that sent servants and gardeners scuttling away in fear of what she might do. "It would put me at ease if you'd be sure that it was nothing dangerous."

"As you wish, My Lady," the man answered. I don't know how Braden felt at the moment, but even I had to remind my fists not to clench.

I tossed him a glance. Instead of looking anxious that we might be discovered, his face went slack as he patted the ground around him. After a moment, he hefted a rock in his palm. I glanced back at the man striding off the trail and straight for our hiding spot. Did Braden plan to pelt him with it? The attack would relieve his nerves but it would confirm Larela's suspicions and give away our location.

I watched Braden, ready to stop him if he tried something foolhardy. He scanned the boughs above us. An almost imperceptible "ah" left his lips before he lobbed the stone into the air.

The rock crashed through the leaves, surprising a hoot out of a large owl. It left its perch and flew directly into the face of the man coming toward us. With a string of words no man should utter in a lady's presence, he dove out of the way. Behind him, the ladies and gentlemen screamed and leapt to the ground as the owl careened toward them, nearly skimming the tallest man's head with its wings before it veered away. Disrupted by the commotion of eight men and women running pell-mell into the forest, half a dozen woodland creatures exploded out of the underbrush and across the path, causing another wave of panic from the ladies as they did so.

Braden peered over the log at the chaos he'd caused. "That went better than I expected," he whispered.

I clapped a hand over my mouth to hold in the laugh that sprang to my lips. The action spurred a silent laughing fit in Braden. Our shoulders shook as the men a few paces away tried to restore order. The ladies' voices rang out, full of panic.

"There was a huge rat!"

"And was that a raccoon?"

"That owl flew right at me!"

I didn't pity the men who had to calm them. Braden and I, hidden from their view by the log, tried to pull ourselves together. Each outburst from the ladies sent us into another laughing fit.

"Enough!" A man's voice rose over the women's hysterics, effectively hushing them. "It was nothing but common animals. No one was harmed. Can we please carry on?" Though couched as question, the statement held more than a hint of command. And irritation.

It was Larela who answered. "Very well, Reggie. But the next time you wish to tarry behind the rest, the answer will be *no*." I pictured her with her nose tipped in the air and her chin held high as she sailed off alone.

"Now, wait—" the voice that had been commanding only a moment ago turned to wheedling. "You know that's not what I . . ." The phrase trailed off as the man hustled after his ladylove, the rest of his sentence lost as he hurried away.

In trying to catch the interchange between Larela and Reggie, Braden and I ceased laughing. As the booted feet finally moved away from us, we sank against the log in relief.

"That was quick thinking."

Braden shrugged. "I told you. I know my way in the woods. Over the years, I found ways of throwing people off my track so I could stay out as long as I wanted."

I didn't want to admit it, but his ploy had been brilliant. The ruckus I'd caused had been blamed on the forest animals; their sudden appearance had put the matter to rest.

"Do you think we should follow them?" Braden asked, peering after the group.

"Do you think that's wise? That was quite a close call."

"If you can refrain from making any undue noise, I don't see why there should be a problem."

If the comment hadn't been warranted by my actions, I would have punched him in the arm. Instead I hauled myself to my feet and brushed leaves and twigs from my clothes. "Then let's go." I offered him a hand.

Braden pulled himself up. "We may as well stick to the path. That was the last of them, and as long as we're quiet," he cast me another admonishing look, "there's no reason for them to suspect that we're following."

A short time later we reached the edge of the woods. The group that included Larela was a good distance in front of us, but they could still be seen from the tree line where we stood. The rest of the group waited for them on the other side of the woods. They reunited after a moment and, at a silent signal, they lined up arm in arm with the gentlemen and filed off toward the town.

Camford, a small village near Lord Bromhurst's holdings, afforded the only entertainment for miles around. However, at this late hour, few lights burned and the various buildings and homes lay still under the summer sky. Dressed as they were, I might have guessed the ladies were headed for the town hall, the only place smart enough to host a dance. From the cover of the trees, we watched the procession skirt the town, following a road that led away from the town hall.

"Where are they going?" Braden voiced my question aloud.

"Only one way to find out." I glanced back and forth to be sure no other traveler emerged before I left the protection of the trees.

"Right behind you."

We reached the place where the company had disappeared in a matter of minutes. Far from the village center with its respectable shops ringing a stone fountain, this area housed warehouses and other places of business. No one came here who wasn't seeking a new horse, some brand of livestock, someone to ship their wares, or a safe place to store them. At this time of night, most of the buildings stood as dark as the homes in town.

"That must be where they are." Braden pointed at the largest building around. It had a low, flat roof and small windows, but unlike its neighbors, the windows glowed with light and shadows flickered across them as people moved about inside. From the music and laughter issuing from the wide doors at the front, a large group—much larger than the dozen couples we'd followed—was in attendance.

Sarah E. Boucher

"Shall we?" Braden asked, already heading toward the entrance. I snatched at his coat and pulled him back.

"Are you insane?" I pinned him with a glare. "Who knows how many of them are in there. I have no idea what you intend to accomplish, but barging uninvited into a room full of people is not the way to go about it."

"Then what do you propose?" He tugged his coat out of my grasp and pulled it smooth.

"We do as we have done all night. We observe, gather information, and then decide what to do about it."

He waved a hand in the direction of the building. "After you."

I relied on the darkness and the gaiety of the assembly to keep partygoers from catching sight of us. Sticking as close to the building as possible, I headed away from the open front doors and around the corner until I reached a window. The length of wall was heavily shadowed. No one would see us. However, a thick layer of dirt and smoke obscured our view as well. I used a corner of my coat to work away at the glass until we could see inside.

"I can't believe it," Braden muttered. Lord Bromhurst's daughters and their companions made up only half of the company. Many other guests, both male and female—who, though not finely dressed as the Master's daughters, displayed the same merriment— were in attendance. A country band had set up in the corner and did their best to keep the audience entertained. Many couples had taken to the dance floor

126

to perform a country dance. If the setting had been Lord Bromhurst's fine ballroom, the dances would have been more formal. I watched Ari spin and weave through the other couples, her feet light, her cheeks pink, and a broad grin on her face, and thought it the best dance I'd ever seen. I imagined thrusting her partner aside and taking his place. Then we would twirl across the boards to the merry tune picked out by the band. The daydream froze in my mind. I was anything but an accomplished dancer. I would probably trip over my own work boots.

"Do you really think this is where they've come the whole time?" Braden said, interrupting my musings. "How has no one found them out? You'd think with all the noise, someone would take notice."

I pondered for a moment before landing on a plausible response. Though not as richly dressed as the sisters, the men accompanying them were dressed finer than the rest of the company. "Someone must be funding the enterprise. The young men escorting them certainly aren't penniless. One of their fathers might own the building, and for the right price, the local constabulary might be persuaded to look the other way."

"So, for *six months* they've been hobnobbing with the local gentry? How have they managed it?"

I looked over the company, noting the glee on the faces of the town girls. "Maybe anyone who finds out is paid for their silence or invited to participate." It made sense. In addition to providing music, someone had taken care to provide long, sturdy tables that bowed under a wealth of cakes, drinks, and other pastries, ensuring that the guests would be well looked after.

"So, what do we do now?"

Braden seemed full of questions tonight, but I had no idea how to address this one. Out from under their father's thumb, the sisters' faces glowed with genuine happiness. The sight both pleased and saddened me.

I shook my head slowly, intently watching the festivities on the other side of the glass. "At present, they're in no danger."

"If by 'no danger' you mean that when their father gets wind of this, if he doesn't lock them in the dungeon, he'll have them all married off within the fortnight, then you're right. And make no mistake, a man of his influence will find out what his daughters have been doing." His eyes were still glued to the scene playing out in the makeshift ballroom. I followed his gaze and saw Larela completing a complicated set of dance steps. She bobbed and dipped with as little care as a child. Braden turned away, his eyes sad. "I suppose beyond informing the Master ourselves, there's little we can do tonight to break up the party."

"And that's unthinkable," I replied.

We watched the women we loved in the arms of other men for another moment. Then we turned away from the window to make our way back through the forest. The weight on my shoulders had grown heavier, the worry for Ari intensifying as my sense of helplessness grew.

"Something must be done," Braden said, falling into

step beside me.

℘ℭ

"Get up."

I cracked open my eyes. Gregor loomed over me with a scowl on his face. After only a few hours' rest, his expression matched my mood. The light of early morning streamed through the window. If it had been my mother, I'd have rolled over and begged for another hour. Depending on her frame of mind, I might have pulled it off. The look on Gregor's face showed he'd make a merciless mother.

I suppressed a groan and dragged myself out of bed. All the bruised bits of my body protested and the beginnings of a headache throbbed at my temples.

"I trust that even with all your gallivanting yesterday, you're fit for work today?"

I held very still. He hadn't been in when Braden and I returned from our trek to Camford and back, but he might have returned earlier and noticed my absence. Best to play dumb. After all, it worked for Loomis. "Gallivanting?"

"Seems every time I dropped by yesterday, you were out. A man only needs to use the facilities so many times a day." He looked me up and down. "Unless he's suffering from some malady."

I prayed the pallor of a night's bad sleep would lend proof to my next lie. "Sickness, you know." I patted my stomach. "Something from the kitchens didn't agree with me."

He sat on the edge of his bed and pulled his work boots on. He considered me for a moment. I tried not to look guilty. It was a good thing he *wasn't* my mother. She'd have seen through the ruse at once.

After a moment, Gregor snatched up a rag and tended to his boots. "What are you waiting for? Today, we work, Jonas." I let out the breath I'd been holding. "After His Lordship's arrival, of course."

With all the comings and goings of noblemen lately, I searched my memory for some scrap of information I might have forgotten. Nothing came to mind. "His Lordship?"

Gregor looked up from his task. "Did no one tell you? The Earl of Gillingham and his son are set to arrive today. As usual, the Master requested that everyone be present to greet them."

I wanted to grumble that he wouldn't miss one measly gardener, but I didn't dare. Gregor had let me off the hook for yesterday. It would be unwise to push my luck further.

I pushed myself up off the bed and began to prepare for the day.

ℴℴ

A fresh shave and a set of clean clothes had revived me somewhat, though under it all, my ribs complained and fatigue continued to drain my energy. As I waited for Lord Gillingham's arrival along with the rest of the staff, ranged in a line in front of the manor, I shuffled my feet as inconspicuously as possible. I had learned during my first few years in service that I could fall asleep on my feet. Gregor wouldn't appreciate that in the least.

I leaned forward to see the ladies standing alongside their father. How could they manage it day after day? I hadn't stayed out as late as they, but the trip through the forest and back had taken a toll. Beyond the occasional twitching of skirts into place, and a yawn emitted by one of the triplets, the ladies appeared to be in fine form.

A ripple of whispers went through the group, and as one their eyes shifted toward the drive where an ornate carriage pulled in. Until now, Lord Mansbury's had been the most gilded carriage I had ever seen. However, this made it look second-rate. Gold gleamed from the wheels to the bits and bridles of the four slim-legged white horses prancing before it. Sunbeams bounced off the glossy mahogany-colored carriage and commanded attention in a way that even the Earl of Candrich's conveyance had not. Every eye fixed on it as it pulled to a stop before Lord Bromhurst and his daughters.

A footman stepped forward to twist the gold handle, swing open the door, and hand out the occupants. First to step down was a gray-haired gentleman with a round, friendly face. He greeted Lord Bromhurst with a broad smile. In a loud voice, the Master presented the Earl of Gillingham to his daughters.

"And this is my son, Lord Richard Comstock," Lord Gillingham boomed, motioning to someone behind him. Fully focused on Gillingham himself, I hadn't noticed the much younger man stepping out. I heard a ripple of feminine murmurs running down the line. They had obviously noticed him. Even the female members of the staff reacted to his presence, some of them with pink cheeks and appreciative eyes.

I glanced back at young Gillingham. He dressed finely enough, with polished knee boots, dark trousers, deep red jacket, gold waistcoat, and white shirt and neck cloth. But he seemed no more attractive than his father. In fact, they looked startlingly alike, save young Gillingham's face was neither wrinkled by time nor as round as his father's.

Lord Bromhurst began introducing his daughters to Lord Gillingham and his son, the father as eager as the son to greet every lady. I tried not to notice how his eyes dwelled on Ari when her turn came, nor how young Gillingham lingered over her hand.

"They say Lord Gillingham himself hopes to find a wife."

I turned to Gregor, not sure if I had heard him right. He wasn't one to gossip or tell tales.

"You think he means to marry one of the Master's daughters?" Uniting with some rich, entitled widow seemed more appropriate. The notion of Gillingham wooing a young lady seemed unbelievable, but the jovial beam in the lord's eye as he met each sister made me uneasy.

"That's what they've been saying," Gregor said. "It's not as if all the Master's daughters are babes."

"Lord Bromhurst would never allow his daughters

to marry someone of his age."

Gregor looked at me out of the corner of his eye, his lips drawn into a line. He knew as well as I did that Lord Bromhurst's estimation of a man had more to do with the size of his holdings than anything else.

When Gillingham and his son had greeted each of the ladies, the duo turned to enter the manor. I prayed Lord Bromhurst would claim Lady Ariela's hand as he had done with Lord Mansbury. Instead, he entered alone at the head of the party. Gregor cleared his throat, as if the Master's behavior proved his theory.

I ignored him. Instead I watched Gillingham offer Ari a courtly bow. Without risking offense, she had no choice but to take his proffered arm. The company made their way inside, Lady Brisella on the arm of the younger Gillingham, and the other sisters following in pairs.

"Perhaps Lord Gillingham has already made his choice," Gregor said, eying me.

I refused to respond to the comment, but that didn't keep it from bouncing around in my skull. I turned toward the gardens. "Didn't you say there's work to be done today?"

෫ᏅᏇ

Normally, daily labor would be a welcome distraction from the issues surrounding Lord Bromhurst and his troublesome offspring. Today, with the sun beating down and the air full of gossip about the goings-on in the manor, I could hardly focus on my tasks. In no time, word had passed through the staff that Gillingham had shown a marked preference for the Master's eldest daughter. I took out my irritation on the weeds while I considered the situation. Ari's kindness wouldn't allow her to treat someone as gentlemanly as Lord Gillingham with disrespect. For once, I wished that she were more like Lady Canela who had to be begged, chided, and bribed to tolerate those she considered unworthy of her attention.

I had to speak with Ari. Age mattered less to Lord Bromhurst than a decent income, and by all accounts, the Earl of Gillingham's income was substantial. For most women that might be enough. The thought of Lady Ariela's youth and vibrancy wasted on a man twice her age bothered me, maybe even more than her interactions with the less-than-worthy village boy with whom she spent most of her nights. At least he was young and showed some sort of genuine regard for her. As refined as he might be, Lord Gillingham knew little more than the beauty of her face and the size of her dowry.

Lost to my thoughts, I missed the approach of two of the Master's daughters and was only alerted to their presence by the shushing of their skirts and the hum of their voices. I trained my eyes on the stubborn weed I'd been hacking at, and moving the hoe in a manner that looked purposeful, I attuned my ears to their conversation.

"Do you really believe she likes him?" It was Lady Daniela, her voice soft and imploring.

"Shh!" Brisella hushed her.

"But have you seen her with him? Her feelings for him are obvious." Could they be speaking of Ari and Gillingham? Had they already formed some type of attachment? I hazarded a look at the two young women. They had stopped no more than five paces away. Daniela's face glowed with curiosity while Brisella's tight lips and stern eyes held censure.

Between her clenched teeth, she said, "Enough of that," and looked pointedly in my direction. Daniela blanched as she followed her sister's gaze, her mouth forming a tiny o.

"So . . . perhaps we should find her," Daniela said loudly, as if reading her lines from a book. "Where do you think Ariela might have gone at this hour?"

Brisella, ordinarily so patient with her sisters, rolled her eyes heavenward as if begging mercy from a higher power. "I believe she was headed to the ruins. She said she needed to think."

"Then we should go find her." Sliding her arm through her sister's, Daniela steered them in the direction of the ruins.

Well.

Their behavior had been as unenlightening as their conversation. Only one thing was clear. If I hurried, I might have time to catch Ariela before she left the ruins.

It was the longest two minutes of my life. I counted them out second by second before stowing the hoe under a nearby shrub and heading in the direction the

135

sisters had gone. If anyone asked why I had abandoned my post, I would claim weariness due to my recent accident. Everyone knew I had spent the previous day on bed rest. Hopefully, no one would argue.

I made my way to the ruins, avoiding the areas more heavily populated by servants and hoping that Ari hadn't left. The whole way, my heart's thumping warned that I would arrive too late. I hurried from the well-tended paths onto the broken stones interspersed with weeds, and my heart finally calmed at the sight of her. Clad in a light dress, she stood with her back to me, her arms wrapped tightly around her. Her stance reminded of the day before when she had backed away from me on the edge of the rose garden. Was she still angry with me for eavesdropping? I froze in place, unsure how to proceed.

She heard my approach and turned. The troubled expression on her face eased a little, the slim wrinkle between her brows softening and her mouth curving almost into a smile. "Jonas, I'm so glad it's you. I was afraid—"

I waited for her to finish, but she didn't. Questions lurked at the back of my mind, overshadowed by her warm welcome. Had she been waiting for someone else? I prayed it wasn't Lord Gillingham.

She took a deep breath and released it. "At any rate, I'm pleased you've come."

A wash of emotions hit me, from pleasure to suspicion. I set the most complicated—jealousy—aside for the moment. All too easily, I fell back into the role of confidante and counselor. "Is there anything that you need, Ari?"

She smiled a small, kind smile. "After yesterday, I didn't know if you would want to carry on as we have always done."

"That was nothing." I kept my tone even. The way she had treated me smarted less in the light of this moment, though the sting was far from gone.

The smile grew broader, with only a flicker of sadness behind it. "I hoped you could find it in your heart to be forgiving."

"I will always do what I can to help you."

The tiniest sound escaped her—something between a hum and a sigh—and her brows furrowed into the expression she had donned before. "I don't know what can be done anymore."

I held myself back. I couldn't bury her in an embrace to ease her tension. She needed space to think. "If you tell me, at least I can share the burden." The offer was safe, neither declaring too much—like the fact that I would do anything humanly possible, including shower her with affection and commit any foolhardy act—nor declaring too little.

"It's Lord Gillingham."

My worst fears crashed in on me, my mind filling with images of them together. I swallowed. "What about him?" I tried to keep my tone light, as if the answer were merely a matter of curiosity instead of the sealing of my fate.

"He's offered for my hand in marriage."

Already? Jealousy rushed through my veins. I pressed my eyes closed to silence its call. When I opened them, I searched her face for some hint of her feelings on the matter. Beyond the faint wrinkle on her brow and the serious tilt of her lips, I could discern nothing else.

"Will you accept?" The throbbing in my veins shoved the question out. The answer wouldn't solve the problems facing her and her sisters. Or me, for that matter.

She took a few steps, sat down on the low crumbling wall behind her and stared down at her hands in her lap. "He's everything that's noble and kind. How can I refuse?"

The words hung between us, squeezing the air from my lungs. I drew in a deep breath and forced my lungs into action. All the pent-up emotions of the years I had spent loving this woman rushed out. "How can you possibly accept?"

Surprise was spelled out in her round eyes. It faded as she pressed her lips together and pushed out a frustrated breath. "Perhaps you haven't been paying attention, Jonas, but no one has offered for my hand in ages. The noblemen who courted me in my glory days never returned after I sent them packing."

The bitterness and anger in her tone caught me off-guard. She had revealed little about her romantic interactions beyond humorous tales that cast her suitors in an unsavory light. I never imagined until now that her prospects had been permanently damaged by her actions.

"Gillingham will be the last, I assure you." The words struck my heart like a blow.

In my eyes, she had lost none of the bloom of her youth. She had only grown in beauty. Were others blind to that? "That can't be true."

With an elegant shrug, she replied. "As far as my father is concerned, it is. He will force me to marry Lord Gillingham just as quickly as he'll force Brisella to marry Gillingham's heir."

"Can't you make him see sense?" Even as I said it, I knew the argument was pointless. Now that Lord Bromhurst had reached his limit, nothing would stop him from doing as he pleased.

She looked at me as if I were mentally deficient. "You know as well as I that once he has chosen his path, there is no dissuading him."

"Then, stop." The words came out before I could think them through.

She met my eyes.

"Stop your nightly escapades or whatever it is you and your sisters are doing. Show him you're the daughter he loves and admires."

Her lips twisted into a grim smile as she pushed herself off the wall and stepped toward me. "Because my sisters are easier to dissuade than my father?" A bitter laugh followed the question. The sound was physically painful.

"You can't carry on this way, Ari. You've said it yourself."

"It's like standing in the ocean tide and begging for it to stop rushing in." She took another step toward me, her eyes burning with a mixture of anger and hopelessness. "Or screaming into the wind and commanding it to cease." With each sentence her voice grew quieter. "Like the sun rising and setting each day, it will carry on with or without me." She crossed her arms over her chest. "There is nothing to be done."

"There must be another way." Where was the woman full of optimism, joy, and an endless supply of schemes? Where was the woman I had grown to love? I desperately wanted to catch a glimpse of her.

Ari looked me up and down with disapproval. "Everybody's hero." Unfolding one arm, she gestured at me disdainfully. "Since you're so keen to fix the world's problems, you figure it out, Jonas."

I held in a wince and tried to dismiss the words, to attribute them to her contrary mood. But the fire in her eyes and the bitter twist of her mouth couldn't be dismissed. Without thinking, I replied, "I'm only trying to help. You knew that if you continued on in this way, you'd be parceled out to the next nobleman who came along."

Her eyes narrowed. "And why do you care about that, Jonas? What does any of this have to do with you?"

I wanted to fling the words back in her face. Hadn't I always been on her side? In even the smallest of troubles, hadn't I stood beside her and offered support? I thought of the man who danced all night with her, who cradled her in his arms. I thought of Gillingham, bending over her hand to kiss it and tucking it through his elbow. If she held any affection for either of them, I no longer belonged at her side, even as a friend. Before I could declare as much, she continued on without me.

"This is none of your concern, Jonas. What happens to me and my family is our business alone. You're nothing more than a gardener, a member of the serving class. Why should our welfare mean anything to you?"

She had never been so cruel. Her heart, in which I had always held a place, was barred against me. I found my tongue and made it form the words that needed to be said. "Of course you're right, Lady Ariela. Thank you for reminding me of my place. Good day, My Lady."

Spinning on my heel, I left her. Anger burned at the back of my eyes. I reminded myself what my brothers would say about men who raged over useless women. I fixed my gaze on the path in front of me and walked away.

Gissela, Hayla & Issela

Just get to work, I reminded myself for possibly the hundredth time as I carried another load of branches to the burn pile. *If she is not the woman you thought she was, why waste your time grieving?* It was a reasonable argument, but no matter what task Gregor assigned me, my heart persisted in dredging up every moment we had shared over the years. Every place on the grounds had been the site of some private conversation or other. When Gregor sent me to the ruins to get rid of the weeds between the broken stones, I relived every detail of our last meeting. Heavy-hearted and engrossed in wrenching plants from the ground, I heard no one approach.

"Jonas," Braden called out in greeting.

I wanted to fling a handful of weeds at him. I refrained. "Aren't you supposed to be in the kitchen gardens, Braden?"

"Yes, I am feeling quite well today too, Jonas. Thank you for asking."

I would not look at him. I would not pitch weeds at his head. "I'd prefer to be on my own today." The truth was, I preferred to wallow alone. The fewer the witnesses, the better.

"So you've said many times over the past week."

I couldn't argue with that. Not only had I avoided Ari and any place where I might run into her, I had also avoided Braden. Nothing could stop the ladies' maids from chattering on about him and discussing the ins and outs of his affection for Lady Larela, but I couldn't stand to hear of it from him. Hope shaped every sentence he uttered and it hit me like a fist to the stomach.

"What happened?" He crouched down in front of me. "Did you behave in an ungentlemanly manner?"

My teeth ground together. The question, framed in that oddly superior tone he affected, annoyed me in at least two different ways. "I'm not a gentleman, Braden. And I'm not to blame. Now get out of my way." Not so long ago, I would have brushed him off and knocked him down a peg or two in the process. Given the determined look on his face, my efforts would prove fruitless now.

Instead of moving, he plopped down in my path and lifted his chin in the manner of someone used to getting his way. "Not until you tell me what happened."

My fist clenched around a handful of weeds and I forced myself to breathe steadily.

"You're my friend, Jonas. If something bad happened, I'd like to know."

The sincerity of his words had no effect on me. I made my voice as flat as possible. "You may either move, or I will remove you myself." I met his eye, glowering at him with all the frustration-fueled rage that had been coursing through my system for days.

He met my gaze, his chin still a fraction of an inch too high for someone in service. "I'd like to see you try."

With that, I pounced on him. Scuffle after scuffle with my younger brothers had trained my body to react to every attack and counterattack. In moments, I pinned him to the ground and began grinding weeds into his face. With outrage twisting his mouth into a grimace, Braden wrenched a hand free, balled it into a fist, and punched me squarely in the jaw.

Stars erupted before my eyes and pain shot up the left side of my face. I clapped a hand to my jaw and tumbled backward.

Braden rolled to his feet and followed me. "I didn't mean to—"

I held him off with one hand, the other still pressed to my cheek.

"It was just a reaction! Something left over from my early training," he rambled. "What can you expect?" He refocused on me. "I really am sorry. Are you going to be all right?"

Early training? I struggled to recall details of his life before the manor, but piecing things together with a rattled brain proved too difficult.

I rubbed my jaw and considered his question. Over

the years I'd been pummeled by my brothers, kicked by a cow, thrown from a horse, and run over by the farm cart. One punch—no matter how well it landed—was nothing in comparison. "I'll survive."

"Is there anything I can do?" He crouched in front of me, looking anxious. "Should I run to the kitchen for some ice?"

As if the cooks would allow their precious ice to be used on a gardener's aching jaw. Heaven forbid some lord or lady was denied a chilled beverage when they expressly requested it. Besides, the pain was beginning to ebb, fading from the initial sharpness to a dull ache. Tentatively, I prodded the point of impact. *Ow.* "I'll be fine," I muttered.

"At least let me finish this job for you."

"Do what you like." I found a length of broken wall overhung with branches from a nearby tree, sat down, and allowed him to finish weeding while I rested in the shade.

True to form, Braden rattled on and on about the comings and goings of the household. I ignored most of it, preferring to stare into space and rub my jaw rather than listen to the same gossip I could have heard from the ladies' maids. Five minutes in, his words snagged at my rattled brain. "Did you say *wedding* preparations?"

"Yes, as I've been telling you, the Master has carried on with his plans for a double wedding."

Surely I had heard him wrong. "A *double* wedding?"

He stopped weeding, swiped his brow with his

sleeve, and squinted up at me. "You haven't been listening to anything I've said, have you?"

He really could be more sensitive than a woman. Scratch that, Ari had never been this sensitive. My heart panged at the thought of her. I took a breath and turned my attention back to the matter at hand. "I'm sorry I haven't been listening, Braden. Please go on."

"Fine, I'll go through it again." With an exaggerated eye roll, he resumed working. "As I said before, Lord Richard Comstock asked for Lady Brisella's hand shortly after his father requested permission to wed Lady Ariela." He let this sink in, working in silence for a moment.

I gathered my thoughts. "I assume Lord Bromhurst encouraged both their suits?"

Braden nodded. "He considers them more than adequate candidates."

"And how did the ladies receive the news?"

"By all accounts, Lady Brisella was pleased with the union."

My eyebrows rose. I searched my memory for a mental image of Gillingham's heir and at last recalled the reserved young man who was overshadowed by his father's bolder personality. Had Lady Brisella shown an inclination toward the younger gentleman? I couldn't seem to remember much after Lord Richard had been introduced to her and she had shyly taken his arm and followed his father and Ari into the manor. If young Gillingham was as well-bred as he appeared to be, perhaps he and Brisella were a good match.

"Lady Ariela, on the other hand—" Braden began.

"You needn't say it. I received an earful on the subject of her engagement to Lord Gillingham."

"She does love him then?" The question was simple enough, but the answer was more complicated.

Ari's demeanor at our last meeting had not indicated any personal attachment to Gillingham, only resignation to the match. If her feelings on the matter had changed since we had spoken, I would be the last to know about it. "I have no idea."

"You spoke with her didn't you? Before putting yourself in solitary confinement, I mean." Braden was more clever than I gave him credit for. If I didn't answer, he would probably hound me until I did.

"Yes." I chose the quickest route to the truth. "We quarreled over it several days ago and she hasn't spoken to me since then."

He turned his keen eyes on me. "Did you seek her out?"

"Because our last conversation went so well? I'm not a complete moron."

"That's what I thought," he said with a note of mild irritation.

Frustrated, I retorted, "Would you have me lap at her heels like a dog?" The twins' comment about my faithfulness to Ari still stung.

He shook his head. "No," he said after a moment. "I would have you court her like a man."

"Wouldn't that be well received by her father," I scoffed.

147

"What does it matter what anyone thinks? If you love the woman, you should assure her of the fact."

"As you have done with Larela?" I shot back.

"The situation with Larela is different. She's only fifteen and I have no desire to complicate the situation any further." I prepared a look of superiority. Before it was fully fixed on my face, Braden added, "When she reaches her majority, you can be sure I will make my intentions known."

This was unbelievable. "You intend to marry her?" Surely that couldn't be what he meant.

"Naturally." The confident tilt of his chin, the set of his mouth, and the seriousness in his eyes was unmistakable.

"And how do you propose to do that? Will you win over her father with your sparkling wit or your dazzling charm?"

He waved a hand dismissively and returned to the weeds. "Time will see that sorted out. What we need to do now is find a way for you to declare yourself to Lady Ariela."

"Impossible. Who would choose a gardener and a life of poverty over marrying an earl and living in the lap of luxury?"

He considered the issue and tapped his chin with one dirty finger, leaving a smudge there. "Consider this: in all the years you have known her, has she held any of her suitors in high regard?"

"No." Ari had poked fun at the gentlemen who'd come calling, and in all likelihood, had been happy to see them driven off.

"And over the years, hasn't she sought out your companionship?"

All the notes, hints, and clues dropped by her or her sisters over the years to arrange for private meetings ticked through my mind. I wanted to argue that it didn't mean anything. The kindness she had shown me was nothing more than a mark of her good nature. "Yes."

"Can't you see it?" He spread his hands before him. "Even from my vantage point, I can see she holds you in high regard." He shook his head. "Besides, both of you have been miserable."

"Both?"

"Yes. You've been unbearable this week and Ariela's spirits have remained low despite her sisters' best efforts."

"Don't hold back," I replied. "What exactly are you implying?" If I said it aloud, I'd never be able to take it back. Ariela could be upset for any number of reasons. What if it had nothing to do with our broken friendship? "She doesn't—"

"She loves you. What other conclusion would explain it?"

The answer came to me at once. "Lord Gillingham. He departed several days ago; maybe she's mourning his absence. Doesn't it seem more likely that she's pining after him?"

Braden rolled his eyes. "Gillingham is a fair old chap, but no young woman has ever favored him. At least not in the last two decades." Having finished weeding, he wiped his hands on his brown apron, rocked back on his haunches, and added, "Also, Ariela's foul mood predates Gillingham's departure."

"What if she's just mourning her lost freedom? Her father *is* forcing her to marry, it stands to reason that—"

"Good heavens, Jonas!" Braden declared. "The woman loves you! How can you not see that? Is it so inconceivable?"

It was. I wouldn't allow myself to even hope that what he said was true. It *couldn't* be true. Ari and I had only ever been friends. Beyond a kiss on the cheek and a hand clasp, the lines of propriety had never been crossed. I had seen to that.

"Then let's go about this scientifically." He walked over and took a seat next to me on the wall.

"What do you mean?" This new, wiser version of Braden was unsettling. I was accustomed to being the level-headed one.

"I propose conducting an experiment. This very night, if it can be arranged."

The strangeness of the whole conversation struck me. Braden's intuition, his logical way of processing and expressing things, differed from his customary manner. "What do you want to do?" I asked, feeling more than a little worried about how he might respond.

"It's not about what I want to do. It's what I want you to do."

My brow furrowed and my lips pulled into a frown.

"Tonight, when Ariela sets out for Camford, you will be waiting to meet her in the woods."

"I will . . . what?"

"You will meet her in the woods," he repeated.

I recalled the night we had followed them to their destination at the dance hall. "It won't work. Ari leads the group. Even if I could find a time to speak with her, it would be in front of all of her sisters and their companions."

"I'd forgotten about that," he said, tapping his chin. "It doesn't matter. Abigail can have a quick word with Larela, and she will take care of that. Leave it to me."

I folded my arms across my chest. "No, it's too risky. I'll find another way."

"You really didn't listen to a word I said, did you?"

I glanced over at him. I had no clue what he was referring to.

"The reason the wedding preparations have been hurried along is because Gillingham wants to be married within the month."

My mouth gaped open like a codfish. Or Loomis.

"Now do you understand?" he said slowly, nodding with each word.

I closed my mouth, the gravity of the situation finally becoming clear. Ari's wedding day loomed in the near future, as certain as if it had already taken place. Staying on at the manor and watching Ari wed a man she did not love would be sheer torture. What would be the point of concealing my true feelings all of these years if she was relegated to a life without love anyway? There was nothing left to lose. I had to try. "You're sure Lady Larela can arrange things?"

"Like I said, leave it to me."

೮ාೞ

The tree-lined path curved before me, bathed in the moonlight of a rising full moon. Stars glittered above, winking between the branches. I reviewed the reason for my visit while I made my way down the path. Tonight I would confront Ariela. Not only would I tell her that I knew what she was doing each night, but I would finally declare my feelings for her. A knot formed in my stomach as I imagined her reaction. I might encounter anything from anger to scorn. My mind whirred between the best and worst scenarios.

Several feet from the path, I concealed myself behind the widest trunk I could find and waited for the party's arrival. I ignored the warnings clanging in my mind, held completely still, and prayed for success. I hardly dared to guess at Ariela's feelings for me. As long as I had known her, I'd believed that expressing my affection would result in rejection, heartbreak, and the dissolution of our friendship. Braden accepted everything so easily, but until the words came from her lips to prove or disprove his theory, nothing would be resolved. My mind continued to spin, and the knot in my stomach grew tighter by the second.

At last, the scuffle of shoes along the path and the low hum of voices both feminine and masculine marked their arrival. Dressed in rich eveningwear, each lady strolled by with a well-dressed gentleman. A thread of fog wove between the trees and lapped at their ankles as they moved past. I pressed myself against the tree trunk to avoid detection.

I caught the first strains of Ari's voice floating on the chill air, near the end of the group instead of the beginning. Was this Braden's doing? I hazarded a glance. Her light hair spilled over her shoulders, and her eyes shone brightly. The contentment on her face was unmarred by the conflict I had witnessed there at our last meeting. The man at her side showered her with acute attention and indulgent smiles. My hands ached to throttle him on the spot.

They stopped a few feet away from me, blocking my escape. Her partner's arm snaked about her waist and they talked like old acquaintances. Jealousy throbbed in my chest like a wound. Ari and I might never share another moment like that. I watched the man lap it up like a dog.

"What do you think of all of this, Jayson?" I couldn't help but peer out at Ari. I was rewarded with a glimpse of her silhouette, rimmed by moonlight. The fog, now thicker than before, swirled about her knees and built at her back. She tilted her face toward the moon.

"Quite lovely," her companion replied. "Quite lovely, indeed." His eyes never wavered from her form, his lips twisted into a half-sneer. My nails dug into the tree's bark, and I considered bounding from my place and throwing him to the ground. I squeezed my eyes shut and clenched my jaw. *Not yet. Not yet.* If I could face Ari without involving this man, I would do so.

Even he could do a world of damage by exposing our relationship.

"Sometimes life can be stifling." My eyes popped open at Ari's words. So sweet, so innocent, and so naive. Lost in her thoughts, she missed the predatory curl of her partner's lips and the dark glint of his eyes. My hands balled into fists of their own accord.

"All sorts of liberties await you, My Lady," he replied. A shiver ran up my spine at the low tone. "You have only to partake."

The tale of a serpent offering forbidden fruit to an unsuspecting maid filled my mind. Had men of that ilk learned no new tactics? My arms began to shake with the effort of keeping them in check. The muscles began to tic in my clenched jaw.

"I just want to live and do as I please. Is that too much to ask?" Ari's words were too light and innocent, too devoid of caution. The unuttered warning hung at the back of my throat, bitter as bile.

"Of course not," the man replied. He ran a finger down her cheek and cupped her chin in his palm.

Would I actually see red next? If he carried on in this vein, I would certainly see the red of his blood spilt on the ground.

"You deserve all the pleasures life can offer." The purr of his voice curdled my stomach. The man leaned forward, pulling Ari closer as he did so. I wondered if I would explode, standing here watching the woman I loved seduced by another.

I tore my gaze from the man to refocus on Ari. Her

154

lithe figure stiffened in his arms. With a hand pressed against his chest—not in invitation but to keep them apart—she said, "I think you mistake my meaning, Jayson." Her serious tone left no room for misinterpretation. She glanced around, possibly noticing for the first time that they were completely alone. I remembered the festivities of the other night, the music, the crowd, the joviality of the group. One couple would not be missed.

I'm here. I willed her to sense my presence.

Unaware that help was so near, her eyes grew wide. At last she understood the danger of her position.

"Never," he said, crushing her against him. "I know exactly what you want." He planted his lips on hers.

The urge to wrench Ari from Jayson's arms and beat the lifeblood out of him was almost uncontrollable. I lunged forward, and then I caught Ari's expression and stepped back. Her face contorted into an expression I knew well: rage. She placed her hands against his chest and shoved so hard that he stumbled backward. His lifted brows and open mouth registered surprise. Ari's eyes burned with the same anger I had elicited only a week ago.

"Do you think that's how a woman wants to be kissed? Hard and demanding, like intimacy is something that can be taken by force?" She swiped a hand over her mouth.

"My sweet," he began, spreading his hands before him. "Did you think that all of this would come without a price? My associates and I have gone to great lengths to ensure that everything is to your exact specifications night after night. We've kept your escapades secret at a high cost." His smile slid back into place. "Isn't this what you've been longing for?"

"No," she answered, warily watching him. "I longed for independence and romance, not being pawed at like a common tart."

He sidled toward her as if she were a wild animal that might bolt at any moment. "Like all women, you don't know what you want." Instinctively, I put all my weight on the balls of my feet, and held my arms at the ready. I would not allow this man to harm her.

Ari retreated. Each backward step brought her closer to my hiding place. I scanned the space behind me for just a moment, then turned back to her. Poised on the edge of the glade, the moonlight bathed Ari's face and the thick fog built at her back. "I do know one thing: I was a fool to think you could offer me anything of value."

Without wasting a second, the man sprang toward Ari. She shoved him away again. He reeled backward into the underbrush, emitting a string of profanity as he did so. At the same moment, I threw an arm around Ari's waist, yanked her back against me, and clapped a hand over her mouth. She thrashed in my arms for a moment and let out a muffled scream, more of rage than fright. I prayed her pursuer was too busy dragging himself out of the underbrush to hear her scream.

"Shhh!" I whispered into her ear. She immediately fell still. I glanced backward again. Five feet away lay a downed tree. As quickly and quietly as possible, I lifted Ari off the ground, took two long strides, and pulled us both into a crouch behind the tree. I hoped Jayson's thrashing and cursing would cover any noise I made. While he struggled to extricate himself from the underbrush, the fog rolled across the moon, plunging everything into dimness.

The racket in the glade grew quiet. "Darling?" The voice, so arrogant before now rang with doubt. "Where have you gotten to, my sweet?" I kept Ari pressed tightly against me, my hand still covering her mouth even though she had made no more attempts to scream or flee.

A roar followed and an explosion of leaves flew in our direction. Apparently Jayson had taken out his frustration on a nearby bush. I checked my arsenal. I had nothing more than my own two fists, still clamped around Ari. If he came any closer, I would have to leave her to attend to him.

"You won't come out?" he yelled as another spray of leaves and twigs landed nearby. "This is how I'm to be thanked for all I have done for you? I have given up everything for you and your precious sisters!"

I craned my neck to peer over the trunk. His silhouette was barely visible through the fog, little more than a tall smudge. Another bush lost its leaves to his anger as he kicked it wildly. Given the way he flailed about, he lacked formal combat training, and, dressed in fitted evening clothes, he would have little freedom of movement for throwing punches, well-aimed kicks, and tackling a man to the ground. The fight would be a short one.

"Have it your way," he growled out. I watched as he straightened his jacket and brushed down his slacks. If he made any move toward us, I was ready for him.

Instead, he threw back his shoulders. "If something befalls you, be it on your own head, Lady Ariela. I'm through with you." His footsteps faded as he stalked away.

I heaved a sigh of relief, my breath brushing against Ari's hair where it hung about her shoulders. She was my primary concern.

The fog rolled away, my heightened concern fading with it. Moonlight bathed the clearing once again. I expected Ari to speak, to express gratitude at the least. Yet something about the way she held herself in my arms—stiff and silent—told me she didn't share my relief. Her pulse racing underneath my palm and her breath so shallow that I barely felt it told a different story.

I took my hand from her mouth, loosened my hold on her waist, and whispered, "Are you all right?" After not speaking for close to an hour, my voice rasped hoarsely. I cleared my throat. "I didn't mean to scare you, but I couldn't stand by any longer."

Only then did I feel the sharp intake of breath. Slowly she turned in my arms until our eyes met. "It's you." The simple phrase was filled with relief, happiness, and something I didn't dare name. The dim light revealed her softened expression, the eyes tilted up at the corners and the lips parted slightly. Before I could gather my thoughts to make an explanation, she flung her arms around my neck. I braced myself against the tree trunk to keep my balance. Ari pressed her lips to mine. My eyes grew wide even as Ari squeezed hers shut and kissed me full on the mouth. My mind shut down and my heart took over. Gathering her in my arms, I poured years' worth of affection, devotion, and love into one deep kiss.

"Jonas," she murmured against my mouth.

My mind floated like a bubble on the breeze. *Wait.* Was she talking to me? Should I respond? The dormant gears in my brain ground into action. "Yes, My Lady?"

"We should have done that ages ago," she said, her breath tickling my lips.

I blinked. Slowly. It took years for my befuddled mind to process her words. "Ages ago?"

"Yes. I've been aching for you to kiss me like that for at least a decade."

"You have?" Reality turned topsy-turvy. I felt as if I'd tumbled into an abyss and had no idea which way was up.

"Oh, Jonas." Her arms moved from around my neck to encircle my chest as she settled her head against my shoulder. I cradled her in my arms, wanting the moment to stretch on forever. "How could you have missed it?"

I thought of all Braden had said. Ari had scoffed at the men who came courting and had sought out my companionship. For years we met in private, and in that time, our relationship had been marked by more than

159

the occasional brush of hands and kiss on the cheek. "I have been blind. Jealous and blind."

She released a sound of pleasure and snuggled deeper against me.

I reconsidered my words. "No. That's not it at all."

At this she pulled back to look up at me, reproach gleaming in her eyes and pulling her mouth into a frown. "Then what is it? Tell me why it has taken you years to realize what is between us, Jonas?"

"I'm a coward." Gazing down at her, I said the words I'd been holding in for so long. "I've loved you so dearly and for so long, Lady Ariela Spencer. I didn't dare believe you could return that love."

Her mouth curved up into the most alluring smile I had ever seen and her eyes snapped with mischief. "Who says I do?"

A growl started low in my throat. Yes, I adored this woman. No, I would not let her trifle with my emotions any longer. I tightened my grip around her and cocked an eyebrow. "I can make you say it."

A giggle sounded as she struggled in my arms, trying to escape. "Not a chance."

"Just remember, you asked for this." My mouth found hers and claimed it. Her struggling ceased, her arms wrapping around me once more. Lost in the moment, neither of us heard the sounds of approach until it was too late.

"I left my dance partner for this? Unbelievable."

Our lips parted with a pop and we turned to see one of the triplets peering over the log. The fog had passed and the moon illuminated the lady's face perfectly, revealing eyes full of disgust and a mouth tucked into a pout.

"Has no one ever warned you about the importance of discretion, Ariela dear?"

Heat rushed to my face. As cool as ever, Ari slipped from my arms and stood to greet her sister.

"Is there something we can do for you, Gissela?"

"Oh, don't concern yourself with me, darling sister." She waved a hand. "Carry on."

If she expected us to resume our earlier activities, she was in for a disappointment. Nothing could spoil the mood like the triplets' interference. I pulled myself up and dusted the leaves and dirt off my clothes.

"What is it you need?" Ariela reiterated. I knew Ari well enough to hear the forced patience behind her words.

"Apparently Lari thought you were in some type of danger. First she told us all to hurry ahead to give you a little privacy and then she came to pieces when Jayson—who was looking more than a little harried, if you ask me—arrived without you."

"So she sent you to find me?"

Gissela examined her nails. "Along with Hayla and Issela, yes."

Ari shook her head. "Now I understand why it took you so long to come to my aid. How much time did you waste arguing before you got here?"

Gissela painted on an expression of innocence and regarded her elder sister with wide eyes. "Whatever

161

could you mean?" Then in a louder voice, she called out, "She's here! I told you I'd find her first!"

Ari scoffed and reached a hand out to me. In a quiet voice, she said, "It looks as if we won't have a moment's peace. You don't mind do you?"

I intertwined my fingers with hers. "As long as you allow me a moment of time later."

"Of course." She smiled up at me.

The other two sisters arrived at that moment, and true to form, they all began arguing. They were nothing like the twins, who spent all their time together and could easily pass for one another. The triplets couldn't be more unlike. With hair from pale blonde to auburn and each girl with a distinct personality, they were only similar in their contrariness.

"I told you I'd find them first," Gissela gloated.

"It's all Issela's fault!" Hayla claimed, glaring at her sister.

"It was not!" Issela retorted. "I'm not the one who fell into the bushes!"

"And who pushed me into them I wonder!"

Issela crossed her arms over her chest and turned away. "I still maintain that it was a badger."

"Why you little—" Hayla began, lunging toward her sister with her arms stretched toward her throat. Issela ducked behind Gissela for protection and Hayla grabbed Gissela's neck by accident.

"Enough!" Ari's voice rang over the clamor. From the fire in her eyes, she was one second away from slapping them silly.

They stared at her with wide eyes, Hayla's hands still wrapped around Gissela's neck and Issela cowering behind both of them. All at once they launched into explanations.

"Hayla is completely out of control!"

"It's all Issela's fault!"

"I'm the wounded party!"

Ari raised a hand and they fell silent. In a voice only slightly louder than usual, she said, "If you will lead the way, we will gladly follow." This was greeted with scowls and more bickering. I listened to them argue over whom should lead the party back, if they shouldn't fetch reinforcements first, or if they should just return home because the evening was already spoiled.

I was grateful God hadn't seen fit to grace my mother with daughters.

"Ladies," taking a cue from Ari, I pitched my voice a little louder than usual. "I believe you will find the path wide enough for all three to pass comfortably." I added a smile and was met with more warmth than Ariela had been. I swept out an arm. "If you would lead on?"

The girls set out and we trailed behind, some part of me longing to linger in the woods with Ari, but knowing that if we didn't keep moving, the triplets wouldn't leave us in peace. When they were far enough ahead that they couldn't hear our conversation, we resumed our discussion.

"So, what did you wish to speak to me about? It's not every day a girl is accosted in the woods in the dead of night." She cocked her head to the side and added, "Twice."

I stifled a chuckle, then took a deep breath. The topic I was about to broach had resulted in an ugly scene a week ago. Braden's advice to address her as a man should echoed in my mind. "First, I have loved you since we met years ago."

From the side, I saw her cheek lift in a half grin. "Yes, I remember it well. You had only arrived at the manor and you had no idea how to talk to girls."

Her teasing was something I'd missed lately. All of our conversations had held an undercurrent of tension. I hoped the lightness would persist, but I had a feeling that as soon as I spoke of weightier matters, it would dissipate.

"Too true," I admitted. "What more would a lady expect of a backward farm boy with no knowledge of women beyond his own mother?"

It was her turn to laugh, the sound ringing out clear. "And yet, you weaseled your way into my heart just the same."

I looked at her, both eyebrows raised. "I told you I would make you say it."

She shrugged one shoulder. "I've said nothing. Only that you weaseled your way into my heart. You'll have to hold out for deeper confessions." She cast a glance at her sisters. They were not that far ahead of us. "When we have a moment of privacy."

A grin tugged at my lips.

"Surely that's not all you came to say," her eyes

twinkled, "when I was out with another gentleman in the dead of night."

I felt the grin fade. "That's exactly what I wanted to speak to you about, Ari. It seems a little inappropriate doesn't it? Sallying off with your sisters to carouse with unknown gentlemen at this unholy hour." Referring to them as gentleman was generous considering they were probably only town folk.

"Carousing?" It was the tone she'd used in our last conversation.

I squeezed her hand and tried to find a way to confront this headstrong woman that wouldn't result in another week of silence and separation from her. "You do understand that I'm worried about you, don't you? I couldn't bear it if this did any permanent damage, either to you or your reputation."

She tossed her head back and laughed. "Oh, you don't need to be concerned about that. Everyone is handsomely paid for their silence. Those that participate in our nightly . . ." She tipped her head to the side, as if trying to think of the correct word. "What might you call them, Jonas? Revels?"

A frown pulled my lips down at the word.

Her laugh rang out once more. "Jonas, I promise you, it's innocent entertainment. Twelve sisters concocted a plan to escape their overbearing father. That's all this is."

It panged me to put a damper on her glee. But I had to say it. "And when your father forces you to marry Lord Gillingham in a week's time?"

The cheer disappeared from her face. "My, you are a fount of information tonight." She pulled her hand from mine to fold it over her chest with the other. "How did this happen, Jonas? In a matter of moments you have plunged us from paradise back into the argument that almost finished our friendship."

This time, knowing that I could fling my arms around her and bury her in kisses to banish the care from her face made the experience all the more poignant. I thrust my hands—which suddenly felt empty—into my pockets. "I can't bear to see you wasted on a man like Lord Gillingham, no matter how kind and gentlemanly he might be."

She turned to me, the worry eased from her face to be replaced with a sad smile. "What are my other options, Jonas?"

I knew what she wanted me to say. Braden would have advised me to declare my intentions, but what was there to offer? As a gardener, I could provide little for her. And as soon as my intentions were made public, I would lose my position and there would be nothing left to offer.

But what if she said yes?

She turned her gaze forward. "What are we to do, Jonas? We keep circling around the same problem." Her arms tightened around her as they had done in the rose garden, as if without their pressure, she might fly apart.

We reached the edge of the forest. The triplets had forgotten about us in their haste to return to their dance partners. Unable to restrain myself any longer, I stepped in front of her and cupped her face in my hands. She kept her gaze averted, looking over my shoulder instead of meeting my eyes. Likewise, her arms remained tight across her chest. I pressed a kiss to her temple and the words rushed out of their own accord. "Would you have me say I would run away with you?" I kissed the other temple and watched her lips flatten into a line. "I'd go this very moment if that's what you want." I brushed the frown with a thumb and dropped a kiss in its place. What was the use in denying what I knew to be true? "I am yours. Command me, and I will do whatever you ask."

At this she broke, her tears spilling over my fingers as she threw her arms around my waist and nestled against my chest. My arms settled around her. After a moment, she drew a shuddering breath and spoke. "Was that a proposal of marriage, Jonas?"

I couldn't think about what we would do with ourselves if she accepted. Her father would be furious when he heard of it. "If you wish it."

Her face, still wet with tears, transformed from gray sky to sunshine, and the widest grin I had ever seen took up residence on her face. She leaned forward, brushing my lips with hers before saying, "I do."

Janela

Regardless of the sun streaming through the window, Gregor's snores didn't abate. I had no clue how Braden had managed to keep him from coming to find me, but from the sounds Gregor produced, I assumed strong drink had once again played a part. I had no wish to wake him, but lay on my back, watching the dust motes drifting through the sun's rays and thinking of the night before.

Lady Ariela Spencer, the most beautiful woman of my acquaintance, had promised to run away with me. I held the thought in my mind and examined it from every angle, hardly believing it to be true. The question of where we might live and how we would support ourselves hung at the back of my mind. If nothing else, my parents would see us provided for, even if it meant living in a manner to which Ari was unaccustomed.

"We will be together, isn't that enough?" she had said. Despite my best effort, her lips refused to say the words *I love you*, but her eyes spoke volumes. Poetry, prose, fiction, and fairytale, all of it was spelled out in those beautiful eyes.

From the angle of the sunlight, I ought to be about my daily labors. Surely I could spare one more moment to dwell on the revelations of the night before.

A moment was all I was afforded. Half rising and emitting a sound like the dead returning to life— something akin to a startled gurgle—Gregor regained consciousness. "Wha . . . ?" Half the word hung in the air, underscored by the befuddlement spelled out in his slack mouth and heavily lined eyes. "Jonas?"

"Yes, Gregor?"

"Oh," he said, relaxing back into his pillow. "Had the strangest dream . . ." He yawned noisily. "You'd run off somewhere in the middle of the night."

My face burned. I swung my legs out of bed and dressed for the day so he wouldn't see it. "Just a dream, Gregor." I retrieved my boots from under the bed and pulled them on. "Are you feeling all right?"

"I'm fi—" He hiccupped, and instead of finishing what he'd started to say, he waved a hand aimlessly in the air instead. "So bright today," he slurred, watching his hand's progress through the beam of light with fascination.

I stifled a chuckle and pulled on my jacket. "You don't quite seem like yourself today. How about I tell the men you're feeling under the weather? I'll make sure everything is taken care of."

"You're a good man, Jonas," he replied, shaking a

finger in my direction. "I'll just lie here for a bit longer." He rolled onto his side, pulling the blanket over his head. A muffled, "Wouldn't mind another few minutes of shut . . ." issued from the blanket. Then the snoring began again.

ℬℭ

Before settling down to breakfast, I ensured that everyone knew their tasks for the day. I stationed Braden at the other end of the property, but since he too had missed breakfast, he followed me to the servants' dining room. Expectancy was written plainly on his face. Before he hit me with a barrage of questions, I figured I would get the first word. "You have a lot to answer for."

"What?" he said, glancing around worriedly. "Why? Where is he?"

"Sleeping it off," I replied, spooning hot porridge into a bowl and grabbing a spoon. Braden grabbed a helping of porridge and settled into the seat across from mine. I'd chosen a table in the corner where we wouldn't be overheard by the groups of gossiping housemaids and kitchen girls.

"How much liquor did they give him?"

"Enough." He dug into his porridge with gusto. "He'll probably be furious when he realizes what happened."

"Not to worry," I assured him, my spoon poised halfway to my mouth. "I'll smooth things over when he reenters the land of the living."

170

He cast me a skeptical look. "I assume all went well last night? You're seven types of chipper today. And it can't be caused by the porridge."

I grinned, popped the porridge in my mouth and scooped up another spoonful.

"Come on, you have to tell me. You have no idea what lengths I went to in order to ensure a private conversation for you and—" he glanced at the group of women still merrily chattering away and lowered his voice to a whisper, "you-know-who."

Gesturing at him with my spoon, I clarified, "The lengths that left you-know-who in a great deal of danger?"

His eyes widened at this. In a matter of minutes, I told him all about Jayson, the triplets, and the part Lady Larela had played.

"What did you say you were doing when Gissela arrived?" The gleeful mischief on his face—more at home on the face of a particularly naughty toddler—goaded me to answer.

"We were having a serious discussion."

He had long since finished his breakfast. He dropped the spoon into the bowl with a clatter. "I'll pretend that I believe you."

I polished off the last of my porridge, licked the spoon, and piled up the two bowls and spoons. Braden's hand settled on top of them. "You're really not going to tell me the rest, are you?"

I answered him with a wide grin while yanking the dishes out of his grasp and handing them to a nearby kitchen girl.

He fell into step beside me as we made our way outdoors a moment later. "You know I'll pester you until you give me all the details."

I thought of the gossiping kitchen girls and housemaids. They had nothing on Braden. "Fine. You were right."

He crowed with delight. "I knew it! I told you she fancied you!" I looked on as he completed some form of victory dance involving prancing around and spinning about. I took a step away and hoped no one else had seen it. When he finished, he clapped me on the shoulder. "I'm happy for you, Jonas. Truly."

I couldn't help but smile. Though embarrassing, his glee was infectious. "When I can, I'll return the favor. As promised." Even though our arrangement had begun with blackmail, Braden hadn't reminded me of our deal for some time. He had also served as a valuable ally. I felt he deserved my assistance.

"All in good time," he replied. "For now, let's focus on you and—" he looked about to make sure no one was listening, "Lady Ariela. Did you come to an agreement?"

"Yes, but since it's between the two of us, it's none of your business." Discussing something between Ari and me with a third party felt disloyal. I preferred to keep our engagement a secret as long as possible.

"The two of you? There wouldn't have been two of you without my assistance. Admit it."

"And I thank you for the part you played in bringing

us together, Braden." I placed a hand on his shoulder. "Now get to work."

"That's not how this is supposed to play out. I risked my job to help you out! Doesn't that mean anything?"

He was right. "Fine. All I will say is that she will not be marrying Lord Gillingham." I let this sink in for a minute. "Now, it's time for both of us to be at our posts." I took a step away, executed a quick bow in his direction, and without waiting for him to protest, headed toward the flower gardens. I grabbed a pair of hedge clippers and a shovel and started pruning the roses and cleaning out the dead brush.

With Braden's interrogation at a close, I could finally plan our elopement. We had been more interested in expressing our affection in a physical sense the night before, so we had made few real plans. One thing was certain; our getaway must take place within the next five days. Otherwise, the double wedding would happen on the sixth. Lord Gillingham was expected to return at any moment. His presence would complicate matters, but wouldn't put a stop to them. The same passageway the sisters had been using to escape the manor could be used to spirit Ari away without anyone being the wiser. Since we were bypassing all the traditional wedding preparations, only two real obstacles stood in the way: my family's cooperation and the acquisition of a marriage license. I could notify my family by letter, though it would take several days and there was no way to be sure they knew of my impending arrival unless I sent a messenger. Since much of our plan hinged on my family's generosity—housing us once we were wed and providing employment for me—it was crucial that the message arrive in time. With little enough ready cash to my name, I didn't dare spend the extra money on a messenger for the full journey and I refused to ask Ari to pay for it. Maybe if I called in a favor, one of the stable boys could be persuaded to play delivery boy and take the message as far as possible. I would talk the idea over with one of them as soon as I had the chance.

That left the marriage license. I had no idea how one might go about it. Questioning Gregor, who in any other circumstance would have been my first choice, would be unwise. It would only serve to awaken his suspicions. Likewise, Braden probably knew about acquiring special marriage licenses—he had been surprisingly knowledgeable on other such subjects—but I didn't think I could tolerate his gloating when I made the request. I would have to find another way to get the information I needed.

Once we had the marriage license, we could escape the manor easily enough, purchase passage on a coach headed toward my hometown, and hold the marriage ceremony somewhere along the way. It would take a couple of days to reach Stohl, so by necessity, our wedding night would also be spent on the road. I paused in my scheming to give it a moment's consideration.

Ari deserves more. The thought raced through my

mind, shutting down the happy thoughts of spending nights with Ari in my arms and days with her at my side. I leaned on my shovel and wiped my brow. Of course she deserved more. Watching her wed someone else would be unbearable, but taking her as my wife and seeing her live in a manner so unbecoming to a lady of her station would also be painful. Why couldn't I have been born to riches instead of being the son of a poor farmer? I could have provided her with the life a woman of Ari's class merited, starting with an engagement sanctioned by her father and a real wedding.

Even though I had been raised in a family of boys, I had spent enough time around the village girls to know that from the time they were young, brides imagined selecting the things that made real weddings: trousseaus, porcelain dinnerware, mounds of flowers, and fancy dresses. Grooms were less particular. As long as the transaction concluded with a blushing bride on their arm, they were satisfied. Sharing a life with Ariela was more than I had ever hoped for, but now that it had become a reality, I wished I could give her more.

"Goodness you look pensive today," a feminine voice sounded behind me.

I turned and came face to face with Abigail. I bowed my head. "Good afternoon, Abigail. What brings you to the flower gardens at this time of day?" The way she shuffled from foot to foot told me she hadn't just happened upon my location.

"Something of a sensitive nature." One side of her

mouth curved up into a half-smile.

"If it's Braden trying to pump me for information again, you can tell him I have nothing more to say." I turned back to the task at hand, moving onto the next bush to clear out the dead leaves and weeds beneath it.

"It's not Braden, Jonas."

I hazarded another glance at her. Her nervous energy had only intensified. "No? Then who is it?"

She pressed her hands against her stomach to keep them still, bit her lip and replied, "Her Ladyship."

With twelve ladies to choose from, I had to be sure which one she meant. "Lady . . . ?"

"Lady Ariela."

Not knowing how much Abigail knew of the situation, I replied, "What could Lady Ariela want with a gardener?"

"I don't have the faintest notion. She only asked me to summon you to the sitting room to speak with her."

Ari had never been bold enough to involve the staff before. Only her sisters had helped her to arrange meetings and pass me messages over the years. Again I wondered how much Abigail knew. "Directly?"

"In fifteen minutes' time." Even though the message had been delivered, Abigail continued to fidget. "She'll be free at that time and indicated that you should meet her at the window."

The situation was becoming stranger all the time. "Thank you, Abigail," I replied, trying to set her at ease. "Please tell Her Ladyship that I'll meet with her at the appointed time."

"Of course, Jonas," she replied. She offered me a curtsy, and as quick as possible, she scurried back to the manor.

I watched her retreat while questions buzzed through my brain. Abigail, though somewhat shy and reserved, had never behaved in such a way in my presence. Ari's request to meet at the sitting room window struck me as peculiar too. What hindered her from meeting me in the flower gardens, for instance? And why was it always my place to do and never to question? Whatever Ari requested, it was my job to comply, even if I found it bizarre, dangerous, or outright wrong. Would the same pattern continue after we were married?

I thought of my parents, both pulling together to run our household and farm. Marriages should be composed of equals. Ari and I had never been on equal ground.

I completed the length of hedge I was working on, shouldered my shovel and hedge clippers, and strode toward the sitting room. Once there, I reassigned the other servants working nearby so that no one else would be underfoot. Then I set up beneath the curtained window to trim the bushes running along the wall. Or at least it would appear to passersby as if that's what I was doing.

Ari didn't appear and I began to feel anxious, wondering if the fifteen minutes had come and gone. I tried to peer into the room, but the curtains were drawn and the window was closed. My stomach twisted into an all too familiar knot.

After a moment, movement on the other side of the glass caught my eye. Lady Janela, one of Ari's youngest sisters moved aside one of the curtains and reached to slide the window up. Daniela, at her side, helped to push it open. Meeting my eyes, Daniela gave me a slight smile.

"You see, monsieur," Janela addressed someone behind her. "It's a perfectly lovely day."

"And if Ariela needs a breath of fresh air, what better?" Daniela added.

What were they up to? The quietest, sweetest, and most studious of the sisters, Daniela and Janela were best friends even though they differed in age by at least five years. Why would these two—the least mischievous of the bunch—be involved in whatever Ari had planned?

A few words grumbled in a strange accent answered Daniela. I dared not glance in to see who it was for fear of attracting too much attention.

Ari spoke from the other side of the room. "That is much better, ladies." Then switching to a more wheedling tone, she said, "Oh dear, monsieur Jacque. I think you were right before. The other veil suits me better."

This was greeted by a heavy sigh and a string of French words muttered in an undertone.

"Monsieur Jacque is always so obliging," another voice added, Brisella, I thought. "We must remind Father to compensate him generously."

The grumbling stopped. "As you wish,

mademoiselle," a tenor voice said, in heavily accented English. "I am yours to command."

Through the window, I caught sight of a slight man with silver hair, a fine mustache, and the apron and impeccable dress of a tailor. After offering a minute bow, he disappeared from the room.

"How long do you suppose we have?" Ari asked, from somewhere out of my line of sight.

"Five minutes, ten at the most," Brisella replied.

"Quickly!" This was accompanied by the rustling of fabric.

"Janela, help me with this wretched train! Daniela, stand guard at the door."

I had no idea what was going on. From the excitement in Ari's voice, I guessed it wasn't bad. Daniela hurried to the door and peered out. Next, Janela shuffled into view, her hands full of white fabric as she backed across the room.

"Careful," she warned, "Jacque will murder you if you do any damage to it."

Then, there was Ari, dressed from head to toe in a long white gown, her face beaming as she peered out at me. "What do you think?"

Words failed me. I stared at her, taking in the long sleeves, the lace and beading on the bodice, and the full skirts I had glimpsed before she had stepped up to the window.

"Do you like it?" she prompted, leaning on the windowsill and smiling beguilingly at me.

"Don't!" Janela cautioned. "If you lean on the sill

you may smudge the gown."

Ari pulled back and checked the bodice for marks.

"Here," Brisella shoved the piano bench nearer. Ari tucked it under the windowsill, sat down, and once again turned to face me.

"If you don't mind, why don't you make yourself scarce?"

"Didn't you send—" I began.

"No," Ari stopped me and fluttered a hand in the direction of her sisters. "I meant them." She turned to address them. "Ladies?"

"I'm in a wedding dress," Brisella retorted. It was probably the only time I'd ever heard her cross Ariela in anything.

"Then go show it off to the others," Ari said, giving her favorite sister a pointed look. "Janela, help her with the train, please."

With various mutterings, they vacated the premises, save for Daniela.

"I'll be waiting right here," she said, taking up her post in the corridor and shutting the door behind her.

Ari faced me once more. "Don't you want to kiss the bride?"

I needed no further encouragement. I squeezed through a slim gap in the hedgerow and pressed myself into the space between the greenery and the building. Leaning over the windowsill, I pressed my lips to hers and breathed in her fresh, flowery scent.

Our lips parted. "Is that all?" she asked with a furrow between her brows. The kiss had been quite brief, especially compared to many we had shared the night before.

I felt a corner of my mouth tug down. "What if I muss your dress? I'm a gardener, Ari. I've been working outside all day." I showed her my hands, the lines darkened by soil.

"What does that matter?" She said, leaning out the window, burying her fingers in my hair and planting her lips on mine.

After a time, she settled back onto the stool and placed her hands in her satin-clad lap. "You never said what you thought of my wedding gown."

My brain was feather-light from the touch of her mouth on mine. I could think of nothing better than, "You look perfect."

Her lips curved up into a grin. "Thank you, Jonas." She leaned over the windowsill, captured my chin in her hand, and covered my mouth with hers. Fireworks exploded behind my closed eyelids and wiped everything from my mind but the wonder of her touch. One thought made its way through and caused me to pull away.

"Isn't this bad luck? The groom shouldn't see the bride before the wedding."

She peered back down at the gown, a tiny pucker appearing between her eyebrows. "Though I do love this gown, Jonas, it's too ornate for an elopement. I'll have to wear something much more suitable for traveling."

My heart tumbled into the region of my stomach.

This was the type of thing she'd be sacrificing for a life with me. I placed a hand over hers where it rested on the window frame. "It doesn't have to be that way. You can still choose this dress, this wedding, this life, everything you've ever known."

Without so much as a flicker of an eyelash, she said, "And abandon my plans of becoming a farmhand's wife? How could you suggest such a thing?"

I stifled a laugh. "I mean it," I persisted. "Life with me will be like nothing you've ever known." I stroked her fingers. "Part of me grieves at all you will be giving up."

"And the other part?" Her light eyes met mine, full of tenderness.

"The other part can't live without you." I lifted her hand to my lips.

"That is all I need to know." She turned her hand in mine to cup my cheek. "A life without . . ."

Would she say it? Would she finally say the fateful word?

". . . affection," she said with a twinkle in her eye, "is no life for me, Jonas."

Apparently, afternoon kisses with a dirty gardener while she donned wedding finery weren't enough to make her confess her love for me any more than midnight kisses in the forest had been.

"They're coming," Daniela popped in the doorway to say.

I pressed one last kiss into her palm before uttering a quick goodbye and slipping back through the gap in the hedges. With a swirl of fabric, Ari vacated her place on the stool to stand and shake out her skirts.

I gathered my tools and strode away. I glanced back at Ari, just in time for her to blow me a kiss.

℘ Q

The following morning, after putting the finishing touches on the letter to my family, I sought out a stable boy I'd spoken with the day before. The servants, those who served indoors and outdoors alike—were collectively running about like a flock of agitated chickens. When I finally cornered Lucas and placed the letter in his dirty palm, I asked what all the fuss was about.

"Lord Gillingham's return. We just received word that he's on his way. We've no time at all to get the stables ready."

"But you will take care of the letter?"

"Of course, Jonas," he said with a wink, "as soon as I can get away."

I left him to his duties and made my way back to Gregor's side. Given the grave expression on his face and the way everyone scurried around him, either he had already heard of Gillingham's arrival or he was irritated about losing a day's work. Probably both.

"We only have a few hours!" He bellowed at Loomis. "There's no time to be wasted by your incompetence!"

Visibly cringing, Loomis shouldered a rake and lumbered off. I feared for the plants in the immediate vicinity. Upset as he was, who knew what damage he might do. I wondered for the thousandth time why he hadn't been sacked.

"What do you need me to do?" I asked Gregor.

He looked me over, his expression showing more than a hint of displeasure. "And where have you been? Lord Gillingham arrives shortly and as usual, Jonas is nowhere to be found." He tossed his hands in the air. "What is it this time?"

"Sorry, Gregor," I hastened to explain, "I needed to post a letter to my mother and the entire staff is in a dither. It took longer than I expected."

Gregor huffed. "Too true. The Master has mandated that the grounds be 'incomparably spotless, shining, and orderly' by the time Gillingham rolls up the drive."

"Implying that we don't generally keep it neat and orderly?"

Gregor mumbled a response.

"Anything I can do to help?"

He considered for a moment. "Don't know anyone unscrupulous enough to do in a nobleman, do you?"

Chuckling, I shook my head.

"That being the case," Gregor said, scratching his head, "if you wouldn't mind supervising the gardeners and groundskeepers, preferably wherever Loomis ended up, it would be much appreciated." He shook his head. "If anyone is certain to makes things worse, it's him."

I asked the question I'd been pondering since Loomis' first mistake made in the first hour of his first day here. "Why haven't you given him the boot?"

With a groan, he replied, "He's Mrs. Jenkins' nephew or some such nonsense. No one wants to risk her displeasure by giving him the heave-ho."

"Ah," I replied, understanding at last. "Nepotism at its finest." I turned to leave, tossing over my shoulder, "If you need me, I'll be between Loomis and whatever stands to be harmed by him."

My comments earned a half chuckle from Gregor before he refocused on bossing the other undergardeners about. To be honest, I appreciated being sent away, even if it meant spending a good deal of time near an unstable man with a rake. At least I would also be armed in a like manner.

₭‑₨

Hours later, the grounds were as immaculate as they should be. Gregor ushered us indoors to wash up and change for Lord Gillingham's return. In due time, we lined up before the main entrance of the manor in the late afternoon's heat.

"So, what do you know about procuring marriage licenses?"

Braden, stationed at my elbow, turned large eyes on me. "Does that mean what I think it means?"

"Shh!" I warned him, immediately regretting my decision to bring up the subject.

"But you are eloping?" Braden asked in an excited whisper.

I sighed. "I knew you'd overreact. Can you help me or not?"

He smirked. "It would be my pleasure. I have certain connections that could make the process quite easy."

His self-satisfaction was almost suffocating.

"It's important that everything is taken care of with the utmost discretion. Understood?"

"Never fear, Jonas. I'll do nothing to put your ladylove in peril," he reassured me with a twinkle in his eye. "Wait. Where are they?"

I looked down the drive. No sign of carriages or any other type of conveyance could be detected. "They haven't arrived yet. You know the nobility, whenever they arrive is exactly on time."

Braden didn't reply. His eyes were fixed on the gaping hole in the middle of our party where Lord Bromhurst and his daughters usually stood. It was peculiar that they hadn't emerged, but given the heat, who could blame them? Sweat trickled down my neck and left a sticky spot between my shoulder blades. The rights of the upper class were boundless. Just once I'd have liked to see Lord Bromhurst labor in the heat of a cloudless day like this. I glared upwards, silently cursing the weather and the noblemen who demanded I stand at attention in it.

"Look!" Braden nudged me in the ribs and gestured toward the main doors. I expected to see Lord Bromhurst and his daughters hustling into place. Instead, I saw the slight form of a lady's maid making her way over to us.

"It's Abigail," Braden mumbled.

As she drew nearer, I could see that it was indeed Abigail, looking more flustered than I'd ever seen her. Braden attempted to greet her. She paid him no heed and stopped directly in front of me. "You need to come with me."

I exchanged a glance with Braden. He, like all the other gardeners, stared openly at the two of us. "What is this about?"

She jerked her head toward the manor entrance.

From her grave expression, I imagined the worst. Lord Bromhurst had been informed of our after-hours activities, or even worse, someone had discovered my secret engagement to his eldest daughter. I shook off all my worries and followed Abigail away from the line of curious onlookers.

We passed through the entryway and mounted the stairs that led to the upper level. Abigail remained silent. I matched her pace as we exited the stairwell and made our way to the family's quarters, my heart growing heavier with each step. I recognized the corridor that housed the ladies' rooms. As we drew closer, a snarl of female voices could be heard, tumbling over one another like a brood of chickens. I grabbed Abigail's arm and pulled her up short before we reached the open door. "Please, Abigail, tell me what's going on."

She shook her head, her mouth pinched tight and her eyes fretful. "He's here, my ladies!" she called out.

I kept my eyes locked with hers a moment longer, hoping she would reveal why she'd brought me here.

After all we had been through together, surely she would tell me something.

"Please," she whispered with a tremor in her voice, "just speak with them."

I took a breath and turned toward the ladies' chamber like a prisoner making his way to the hangman's noose. I stepped over the threshold to the ladies' sitting room and paused inside the doorway to get my bearings. On every side, perched on every available piece of furniture, sat His Lordship's daughters, dissimilar in height and coloring, but alike in the accusatory glare they all wore. I wanted nothing more than to leave the room the moment I entered it. I held my ground for one reason only: Ariela was not among them.

I offered an awkward bow and addressed them as politely as possible, while my concern for Ari's absence grew. "Ladies. Is there some way I could be of service?"

"You *would* act innocent," Lady Canela's words cut across the silence.

"Pardon me, My Lady?"

"Don't pretend like you have no idea what I'm talking about. We all know about your relationship with Ari."

Silence once again claimed the room. I fidgeted internally and did my best to stand erect under the weighty stares of eleven angry women. No. I recalculated. There were only ten. A quick glance revealed Lady Brisella's absence.

"Give him a moment to defend himself," one girl called out. I turned to face the speaker. It was Janela. "I've seen him with Ari. He'd do nothing to harm her."

"Harm her?" I repeated, my tone more defensive than I intended. There was already enough hysteria in the air. I calmed myself before saying, "I would never do anything to hurt any woman, especially not Ariela."

None of them batted an eyelash at the use of her given name or the omission of her title.

"Where is she?" I feared the answer, but I had to ask the question.

Canela crossed her arms over her chest, tipped her chin up, and glared down at me. "You tell us."

"I haven't the slightest—" I began, looking around for support. Though not everyone looked on me with the same hostility of a few moments before, no one came to my aid either. I cleared my throat and ordered my thoughts. "I haven't seen her since yesterday when she summoned me to the sitting room window."

Daniela, who had likely caught much of what had passed during my last meeting with her eldest sister, nodded. "And then?" Her voice was soft and entreating, holding none of the condemnation Lady Canela's had. "What of the letter?"

Letter? My confusion and alarm for Ari's safety increased by the second, I spread my hands before me. "What letter?"

A reply came from behind me. "The letter you passed to Lucas this morning." Abigail, standing in the doorway, met me with set lips and hard eyes.

"Do you deny it?" Canela demanded.

I shook my head, turning back to face her. "No. I asked one of the stable boys to deliver a letter this morning. Is that important?" Had someone intercepted the message to my parents and learned of our plans to elope? My worry intensified when Larela stepped forward with a scrap of paper in her hand. She placed it in my palm. "Is this it?"

From the smooth texture of the sheet, I could tell it wasn't the letter I'd sent to my family. The paper available to the servants was coarser. With a feeling of relief, I turned it over. Ariela's name was scrawled across it in a bold hand. "The letter I gave to Lucas was addressed to my family. This isn't it."

The room dissolved into chaos once more as exclamations of distress and disbelief filled the air. Larela's voice, strangely quiet and calm, sounded in my ear. "Please read it."

I unfolded the letter, doing my best to control the tremor that had begun in my hands. A single sheet of paper as fine as the scrap Ari had used to tell me to meet her in the ruins, it held only a few words:

Meet me in the forest at dawn, my sweet.

-J

"I don't know who wrote this," I said, staring in disbelief at the words, "but it wasn't me."

Larela rested a hand on my arm; her normally cheerful countenance had grown serious. "I think I do." Clearing her throat, she addressed her sisters loudly. "Jonas had nothing to do with this."

A few choice words were uttered. Daniela shot Canela a quelling look. Canela fell silent, her lips pressed into a pout.

"Here is what we know. Sometime during the night or early this morning, this letter arrived in our chambers. Apparently," here Larela looked at Abigail, who ducked her head to avoid the attention, "no one noticed who delivered it. Jonas's very presence is testament to the fact that he had nothing to do with Ari and Bree's disappearance."

"What if he had a darker plan in mind?" One of the triplets, Issela I thought, asked.

"Yes!" For perhaps the first time in her life, Gissela agreed with her sister. "What if he carted her off to do *unspeakable* things to her?"

"Ooooh . . ." Hayla joined the action, pointing at me excitedly. "He does have a fondness for snogging in the woods!"

Frustration settled over me. With all this banter, how could I ever find out what happened to Ariela and Brisella?

"Don't be ridiculous," Daniela silenced them with quiet censure. "How could he snog her when he's here with us?"

"Exactly." Larela took control of the room once more. "We can assume that Ariela believed the letter to be from Jonas from the things she took with her." Here she turned to me, "We can assume she thought she was running away with you."

My heart thumped while my mind tried to make

sense of it. "And Brisella?"

Her lips drew into a grim line. "She would never have let Ari go alone and Ari would never go anywhere without telling her."

"No one saw or heard anything out of the ordinary?" I asked, hoping that the answer would not be in the negative.

"Nothing," Larela shook her head. "But now that you're here, I believe I have a good idea what happened."

Swiftly, the pieces fell together. "I do too." I spun on my heel. "There's only one way they could have escaped unseen. Abigail, fetch Braden and Gregor as quickly as possible and meet us outside."

"Wait!" Everyone looked at Krisela, who hadn't spoken until then. She hurried across the room. "I'll go with you, Abby." Without losing another moment, the pair hustled out of sight.

I made my way across the room to the hidden corridor. "Pardon me, ladies." In stunned silence, they watched as I fingered along the wall until it sprung open. Warm, stale air flowed through the opening.

"How did you know about that?" Canela asked.

I faced her, unable to keep one side of my mouth from pulling up at her annoyance. "You'd be surprised what I know, Lady Canela."

"What about my father?" Canela asked in annoyance. "He's already upset that we refused to come down! You can't just expect him to sit still when his eldest daughters have gone missing."

"Stall him, Cinnamon," Larela said. "Getting him involved will ruin everything."

"We'll handle it," Daniela appeared beside Canela. "Just bring them back safely."

"Hold it!" one of the triplets called out. "If Jonas didn't do it, then who did?"

"Jayson Kemp," Larela answered flatly.

The women gasped, exclaimed that they'd known it all along, and fired questions at one another all at the same time.

"Here Jonas, you'll need this." I glanced down at Larela, poised at my elbow with a lamp in hand. "And I'm coming with you."

Krisela

The triplets fell to speculating on what had happened to their elder sisters. An argument ensued instantly. The panel clicked shut, muting the cackling henhouse on the other side. I rested my palms on the wood and blew out my breath slowly. Quiet enveloped me like a blanket.

"Well? What are we waiting for?"

I cast Larela a glance. She was doing everything but tapping her toe impatiently. "Sorry. Just gathering my thoughts after that inquisition."

"You seem to have survived," she said, starting down the stairwell. The lantern in her hand cast long shadows across the walls and illuminated the landing where Braden and I had hidden over a week before. "Coming, Jonas?"

"Shouldn't we wait for Braden and Gregor?" I asked, falling into step with her and swiping a hand over my sweaty forehead. The afternoon heat made the stairway muggy.

"No," Larela said, looking cool and calm. "The girls will tell them where we've gone. If I know Kris, she'll have guessed already. She'll lead them to the tunnel's entrance."

"Clever."

"Speaking of clever, how did you know about the hidden door?" She stopped on the landing and arched a slim eyebrow up at me.

I stopped. I needed an explanation that didn't include peeping in her window like a fiend. "Braden and I discovered it."

She let out a sound of disgust. "That boy's curiosity is revolting."

With a sidelong glance, I noted the too-pink cheeks. "Hmmm . . . I see he wasn't exaggerating. One can never tell with Braden."

"Excuse me?" The tone of her voice verged on annoyance.

"With five younger brothers who liked to turn girls' heads, I've learned to spot the signs. Abigail becomes both shy and overly bold around Braden. You, however, are irritated by him." I ignored the outrage deepening the color in her face, took the lamp from her hand, and led the way down to the tunnel entrance.

"Of course I'm irritated by him! Have you seen the way he behaves around every girl who crosses his path?" I looked up at her, still poised on the landing, her hands propped on her hips and her eyes flashing.

"It all comes to the same thing, My Lady." I

continued downward, doing my best to ignore the sweat sticking my shirt to my back. At least I hadn't brought a jacket this time.

After a second, her footsteps struck the steps with a sharp tip-tap. "And what, pray tell, does that mean?"

Ari and I often engaged in this type of verbal contest. I reminded myself that the tact and patience possessed by the elder sister probably hadn't developed in the younger. Baiting her wouldn't be kind or productive. Besides, there was the deal I'd struck with Braden to consider. If I carried on in this manner, it wouldn't help his case.

I waited until she drew up beside me on the stairs and met her eye. "It means you are fond of him, Lady Larela."

"What utter nonsense," she said, snatching the lamp out of my hand and pushing past me. "And stop calling me Lady. Lari will do. Or Larela if you prefer."

"As you wish." I offered her a minute bow. "Maybe I'm mistaken," I added for her benefit. Maybe she hadn't fully realized her feelings for Braden yet. But after seeing her reaction firsthand, I had no doubt about how she felt for him.

"Besides, what does it matter?" She turned to peer up at me, her chin held as high as Canela's had been a few moments ago. "He pursues anything wearing a dress."

"He's young and foolish, it's true. But he knows what he wants and he's willing to work for it." I remembered our recent conversations. He had vowed to make his intentions known at the right time.

"And what is that exactly?"

"You."

The effect of that one word cut through her defenses, the line of her mouth softening.

When she didn't reply, I said, "I have no idea when he plans to make his declaration publicly, but you are all he ever speaks of. No matter how it may seem, he has eyes for no one else."

The anger drained from her face. After a moment, she swiped a hand over her eyes and cleared her throat. "My sisters have gone missing, one of whom is your fiancée, and here we are discussing that stupid gardener."

"We'll find them." I promised.

We continued on in silence for a few steps.

"What do you think happened to my sisters?"

"The man who's been meeting Ariela in the woods each night, what was his name?"

"Jayson Kemp."

"How did he behave after Ari disappeared the other night?"

She considered for a moment. "He wasn't pleased. When Ari didn't return, he stormed out. Do you think he means her harm?"

I remembered how beastly he had been in the forest when Ariela had rejected him. Not wishing to add to Larela's alarm, I kept my face blank. "If he meant what he said in the letter, maybe not."

"And if the letter was a ruse to get her to meet with

him?"

The same thought rested like a rock at the bottom of my stomach. A large jagged rock. "If that is the case, I'll make him answer for it."

"Good."

By this point, we had reached the underground tunnel. The temperature dropped and my physical discomfort eased somewhat. On the other hand, my mind continued to conjure up the many horrible things Jayson could be doing to Ari at that very moment. Remaining as composed as possible for Larela's sake proved more difficult by the second.

With Larela setting the pace and warning me of pitfalls in our path, we proceeded quickly and without any of the mishaps Braden and I had encountered before. The staleness of the air and darkness of the tunnel lightened when we neared the vine-covered mouth of the cave. I brushed the vines aside and held them in place while Larela passed through.

Hoof beats could be heard approaching as she stepped into the glade. A familiar voice called out her name. I stepped out in time to see Braden riding up to her with a relieved look on his face.

"Did you find anything in the tunnel?" he called out.

She shook her head. "Nothing."

"I'd hoped there would be some clue as to what happened." He cleared his throat. "No matter. We'll find them soon enough." He put on his most reassuring smile and extended a hand to Larela.

"Why don't I get my own horse?" I recognized the tone. It was the same one Larela had used on the stairs. All the anger of twenty minutes ago flickered in her eyes.

"Your father thinks Ariela and Brisella have wandered into the forest on a whim, thanks to Canela. We couldn't very well take a large party into the woods to bring them back without raising suspicion, could we?"

Larela glared up at him with her mouth pursed.

"Don't you want to find your sisters?"

She huffed and hesitated for a fraction of a second longer, anger and annoyance flitting over her features. Finally, she placed her palm in his and let him pull her up behind him. The grin on Braden's face was almost unbearable. The words *I told you so* were practically scrawled across his brow. At least Larela couldn't see it.

Two hounds, one brown and the other black, bounded up to Braden's horse and frisked about its knees. Gregor and Krisela cantered up on their own horses and with another in tow.

"Jonas," Gregor greeted me with a curt nod. He tossed me the reins of the third mount.

I snatched them from the air, mounted quickly and fell into pace beside Gregor. "What have they told you?"

"Enough," he grunted. "And little that I didn't already know."

Inwardly, I blanched. I didn't ask him to elaborate.

At best, his knowledge of my involvement with the ladies would result in a stern lecture on propriety, and at worst, physical punishment and the loss of my position. And possibly a limb or two.

"Relax, Jonas," he said gruffly. "I'm not going to tan your hide today. But just remember, discretion has never been your strong suit." With that, he pulled ahead of me, letting his horse fall into step with Braden and Larela's. I slowed my pace until Lady Krisela was close enough to speak to.

"What did you tell him?" I asked in a harsh whisper.

Her cheeks pinked. Of all the sisters, she was the most reserved, feeling more at home with animals than people. When she spoke, her voice held none of the confidence it had when she'd bounded across the room to stop Abigail. "Hardly anything. Abby told him the girls were missing and he sprang into action."

Involving Gregor had been a gamble. I had only done so because no one handled an emergency better than he. The fact that he hadn't gotten after Braden when he'd swung Larela into the saddle proved that Gregor knew more than he was saying.

"Thank you for bringing him," I said.

"They're my sisters—" Lady Krisela began, but the rest of the phrase was lost as the dogs began to bay.

I snapped the reins, urging my horse forward, and guiding it to the place where the dogs yipped and howled beside the trail.

"What is it?" I called to the others, who had already

dismounted.

Braden held up a cloak and asked Larela, "Is it one of theirs?"

She motioned for him to pass it to her and when he did so, she inspected the garment. "Yes, it's Bree's. Without a doubt." She handed it to her sister.

"It's damaged," Krisela added, holding it up to show a long tear parting the fabric.

Everyone fell silent for a moment, the jingling of the horses' bits and bridles loud in comparison.

"At least now we know we're on the right track." I shared a glance with Gregor, whose face was grim. "And there's no time to waste." I pulled my mount back onto the path and started forward again, my mind filling with horrible images.

"Any idea where he might have taken them, Larela?" I tossed the words over my shoulder, earning a stern look from Gregor for failing to use her title. After spending the better part of an hour traipsing through dark tunnels and back staircases in her company, it felt unnecessary.

"I'm not sure. I'm not even sure if he lives in town."

"What's the boy's name?" Gregor butted in.

"Jayson Kemp," Larela answered.

Gregor scratched his jaw. Being born and raised in the area gave him a surer knowledge of the townsfolk than I. "Is his father in trade?"

"I believe so."

"Then he would be Anthony Kemp's son, I assume.

The family lives on the west side of the village. If we find no further clues, we'll start there."

"Lead on." I motioned him forward.

As he passed, he spared me a look of disapproval. "You and I will talk later."

Yet more joys to anticipate. The future, which now included the certain loss of my position and a tongue lashing from Gregor, looked bright indeed. If only Ari and her sister were spared by my actions, it would be worth it.

Though we searched carefully, listened, and watched for any indication of where they might have gone, no further clues could be found. The dogs snuffled along the path beside us but found nothing else. When at last we reached the edge of the trees and rode into the unfiltered sunlight, Gregor turned his horse toward the west.

Braden caught my eye and jerked his head in the direction of the warehouse. I motioned toward the dogs, who still nosed along the trail but showed no inclination for east or west. I shrugged and turned my mount to follow Gregor in the opposite direction. The rest of the party trailed behind. Within a few minutes, we reached wide streets lined with quaint, brightly painted houses with well-tended yards. Other than children playing on one side of the street and an old woman with ratty white hair working in her garden on the other, no one else could be seen. We stopped before the house where the children were playing. It was a neat enough home with a red door, shutters, and a white picket fence.

Gregor called out to the children, "Does Jayson Kemp live here?" His voice, loud and authoritative, sent most of them scurrying inside.

One child had reached a hand through the fence to pet the black hound. She turned her large brown eyes up to Gregor. "Yes, sir." The words came out in little more than a whisper.

"Is he at home?"

She shook her head.

"Do you know where he's gone or when he'll return?"

She shrank more with every question, her eyes growing larger by the second. Her words were barely audible. "No, sir."

Gregor's lips curled into a kindly smile, pushing the wrinkles that surrounded his eyes and lips into something more grandfatherly. With one hand, he searched his pockets. He pulled out an apple and tossed it to the child. She snatched it out of the air and clutched it to her chest.

"Are your parents at home?" Gregor asked.

"They've gone to market." Her voice was timid, but the fear had drained from her eyes.

"Thank you, my child," Gregor said.

Her head bobbed in a nod before she scrambled after her playmates, the apple clutched tightly in her fist.

"Now what should we do?" Braden asked.

"Pssst!" the old woman hissed from across the street. "You're looking for Jayson Kemp?"

"Yes, my good lady," Braden answered, with his most congenial smile.

She clicked her tongue. "That boy is up to no good. Comin' and goin' at all hours of the night. It's indecent."

"Have you seen him today?" I asked.

"Seems he was gone earlier than usual." She scratched at her mess of hair while she thought. "Oft times nobody sees him up and about 'til late afternoon. Today 'twere around dawn."

"Could you tell us, good lady, if he was alone?" Braden posed the question.

"I b'lieve so," she replied, her lips twisted with disgust. "Though he always runs about with those rough town boys. And the no good girls too, goes from one to t'other like a pig in the mire."

I had disliked Jayson from the first moment I'd seen his arm snake around Ari's waist. Hearing of his reputation only confirmed my suspicions. I tried not to dwell on what such a man might do to Ari and ignored the rocks multiplying in my stomach.

Gregor, quiet until now, asked the old woman, "Does Master Kemp keep a warehouse?"

"Yes, sir," she replied, treating him with a deference she hadn't shown Braden or me. "The large 'un on the other side of town."

Braden caught my eye and raised his brows. I shook my head ever so slightly. The less Gregor knew of what had been occurring over the last six months, the safer the ladies would be.

"Thank you, ma'am," Gregor replied, flipping her a coin for her troubles.

"My pleasure, young man," she flashed a sparse-toothed grin at him before pocketing the coin.

୫୦୦୨

We followed the route through town toward the trade quarter of Camford. Beyond the regular traffic—market goers weaving in and out, peddlers hawking their wares, children playing in the streets, and carts and wagons maneuvering their way through all of it—nothing stood out as odd. Larela recognized one or two of the young men from the ladies' nightly escapades. We questioned them about Jayson and his whereabouts, but no further information could be gathered. Leaving the bustling town center behind, we entered the quieter area on the outskirts of Camford that boasted nothing more exciting than row upon row of broad warehouses. The streets were almost empty. With the sun dipping over the horizon, merchants would be closing their doors to the public and settling their accounts. The time for business had passed.

"This is it," Gregor said at last. Larela and Krisela shared a glance. None of us said anything. Instead, we stared at the large, flat-roofed building that at least four of us recognized as the site of their midnight revelry.

"This is where you come, isn't it?" Gregor said. Had he expected an answer, Larela's stunned expression would have been enough. "I thought as much." He dismounted and the rest of us followed suit.

"We should have come here straight away."

"Wait." Larela said. "How did you know?"

He waved off her question. "There will be time for explanations later." He turned his disapproval on me, his mouth set in a grim line. "This is your rescue mission, Jonas. Now that we're here, what do you propose we do?"

The whole group turned to me. I ignored the men's stares and the expectation in the women's eyes that threatened to paralyze me. Regardless of what Ari had said, I was no hero. I took a breath and pressed my eyes shut. I weeded through my thoughts, discarding those that would be of no use to me. To Ari. Her welfare was in my hands now. I focused on the dogs, who were nudging Krisela in the direction of the warehouse.

"The wisest course of action is to split up and search the perimeter. We don't know if they're alone or if Kemp brought reinforcements. It would be foolhardy to barge in without learning as much as we can first." I pictured Braden or Larela, the most impetuous of the group, barreling in without a second thought. "No one is to enter the building unless instructed to do so by Gregor or me. Is that understood?"

When everyone had indicated that they would do as they were told, I continued, "Braden, take the north side, Gregor take the south, and the ladies and I will take the west side." The west included the main entrance facing the street, which I deemed the safest way to approach.

"Lari is coming with me," Braden said, while

Krisela pointed out, "That still leaves the east side."

Larela narrowed her eyes at Braden though no protest crossed her lips.

"I'll take the dogs and inspect the east side," Krisela said quietly, reaching down to pat the hounds' heads. Seated at her feet, they gazed up at her adoringly. "We'll be quiet, won't we, boys? And you'll keep me safe?" The two dogs nuzzled her thighs in response.

"It's settled then," Gregor said, grabbing the reins of all four horses and securing them to a nearby hitching post.

Krisela snapped her fingers and the dogs fell into place at her heels. Together, they headed around the left corner toward the rear of the warehouse, Krisela snapping her fingers when they let out as much as a whine. Braden drew Larela's arm through his and led her toward the right. I glanced at Gregor to see if he had noticed. He had already disappeared around the left side of the building, dutifully carrying out his assignment. I released a breath I hadn't realized I'd been holding and began my own inspection.

The front of the building boasted nothing more than the heavy double doors that opened wide enough to accommodate a wagon. The rough planks fit the doorframe, but left gaps large enough to peer inside. The wood floor showed dusty footprints, leftover bits of food, lost feathers, and even a forgotten handkerchief. Telltale signs of the last dance. The interior that had gleamed with candlelight late at night seemed dreary and dull in the afternoon.

Though the next gap was larger, it provided nothing more enlightening. I was about to move on when a flash of movement in a far corner drew my attention. I watched carefully and hoped for another glimpse.

A bright whistle caught my ear. After one last look through the planks, which revealed nothing, I made my way around the right corner of the building. Gregor, close beside Braden and Larela, stood by the rear of the building and peered through a small window. Gregor caught sight of me and motioned for me to approach. At the same moment, Krisela and the dogs rounded the other corner and joined them.

Breaking into a jog, I hurried to them. "What is it?" The thumping of my heart, due more to my heightened anxiety than the jogging, banged in my ears.

"Look for yourself." Braden moved out of the way so that I could see inside. On the other side of the glass paced a lone figure in a long cloak. Each jerky step spoke of agitation. A thin voice spoke from somewhere near him. He turned toward it.

"Shhh!" I flapped a hand to hush the others, tuning my ears to the slightest noise. Braden rolled his eyes but didn't say a thing. The man's voice could be heard plainly enough, even through a pane of glass.

"Months I've invested in this venture, and this is all the thanks I'm to receive?" I recognized the voice, even if the shadowy figure was barely recognizable.

Someone answered him, but it was impossible to make out the words.

"Can you appreciate the lengths I went to for you? I

satisfied your every whim and paid off any who came to know about the high and mighty ladies' doings. I kept the secret as if it were my own." Jayson Kemp threw his hands in the air. "I kept it from public knowledge for the better part of a year!"

Another thin response threaded through the glass. I strained to recognize the voice, but it was too hushed. Impatience warred with the rage growing inside me. I scanned the room for possible entrances. Other than the wide doors at the front, a single back door served as the only other means of entry. Kemp paced about twenty feet away from it. I wondered how quickly I could get through the back door before he could harm his captives.

"It's not good enough!" My attention snapped back to Kemp. He approached the darkest corner of the warehouse and squatted down. When he spoke, his tone was lower, more controlled, but somehow more threatening. "If I can't have you, at least I can take your father's money and your good reputation!" The words caused my stomach to churn.

With something like a snarl, Braden lunged toward the back entrance. At the last second, I yanked him back by the collar. "Did you forget what I said?" The words were sharp. Sharp enough to hide the fact that barging in and beating Kemp to a pulp had been my first impulse too. More calmly, I said, "We gather information. Then we develop a plan."

Braden's wild eyes and too-loud tone conveyed his feelings on the matter. "This is a time for action, Jonas!

Do you propose that we sit here and do nothing?"

Gregor folded his arms over his chest and quelled Braden with a glare.

I released Braden's collar. "First of all, there's a lock on the door," I gestured toward the back entrance. "Trying to barge in that way will only alert Kemp to our presence and give him plenty of time to either harm them or escape."

Braden mumbled something about how he could handle the lock.

"Second," I continued as if he hadn't spoken, "If you don't think I want to charge in and flatten that useless excuse for a human being to the ground, then you're wrong. As far as I can tell, the ladies are alive. I'd like to keep it that way." I turned to face the rest of the group, "Did you see anyone else on the property? Or any evidence of weapons?"

"No," Braden replied sullenly. "There was no one else."

"And unless it's on his person," Gregor added, "there aren't any weapons nearby either."

"We have to assume he is armed. Otherwise, why would the girls have gone with him so easily?" Larela said.

"That's a chance we'll have to take."

℘℘

"Are you sure you can handle the lock?"

Braden sent me a scathing look. "I said I could do it."

"Without alerting Kemp to our presence?"

"Yes, for the fifth time. I can do this, Jonas." Agitation flashed across his face and his nostrils flared as he knelt before the back entrance with his hand poised over the lock.

From this close, we could hear movement inside the building. Apprehension tugged at my stomach while impatience wrestled in my chest. I wanted to tell Braden to set to work, but it was crucial that we wait for Krisela's signal. Acting out of turn could result in injury to those we planned to rescue.

"What is taking so long?" Larela muttered at my elbow, as anxious as I to get this over with.

With as much calmness as I could muster, I replied, "Give them another minute."

In less time than that, the clamor began. Dogs barked, the thunder of several sets of hooves sounded, and then came a loud splintering of wood.

"Now!" Larela urged Braden.

He had already begun fiddling with the lock. In a matter of seconds, the knob twisted in his hand, the door sprang open, and we crowded into the warehouse. Instead of looking toward the center of the room where horses, men, and dogs mingled in a cloud of dust, I scanned the nearest corner for the two women.

My eyes fixed on Ari, her hands and feet bound and a gag stuffed into her mouth. Fierce affection, relief, and rage washed over me. She stared up at me with wide eyes, more helpless than I had ever seen her.

Ten steps forward and I scooped her into my arms

to carry her out the back entrance. I breathed in the scent of her. Her usual clean scent was muddled with dust and the sharp tang of fear. My anger intensified. I set her down a safe distance from the building, loosened her bonds, dropped the gag to the ground, and shoved the ropes into my pocket. With rage pushing me forward, I turned to reenter the warehouse.

"Jonas!"

I glanced back at Ari.

"Please don't leave me." The plea was at odds with the independent woman I knew and loved. I looked her over from her dirt-caked hem to her mussed curls. Little would be more rewarding than staying by her side and banishing her fears with kisses, but the barks, thuds, and raised voices emanating from the nearby building reminded me that there was still a job to be done.

I cupped her face in one hand and pressed a kiss to her forehead. "I need to know that you're safe. I can't do that if Kemp isn't taken care of first."

She wrapped a hand around my wrist and squeezed tightly. Some of the old fire flashed in her eyes. "Then, give him what he deserves," she said before releasing me.

A grin pulled up one side of my mouth. I turned away from her to reenter the building. Braden, with Larela at his heels and Brisella in his arms, passed me as I stepped toward the door.

"You might want these as well." Larela handed me the ropes that had bound Brisella.

I shoved them in my pockets. "Stay with them," I

instructed Braden, "and whatever happens, don't let any of them back inside." Hopefully, the commanding tone wasn't lost on him.

The chaos that had allowed the three of us to enter unnoticed had abated slightly. Stepping through the door, I witnessed Gregor and Krisela's handiwork. The wide front doors were hanging open, spilling a broad rectangle of light on the scene. In the center of the floor all four horses whinnied with excitement, their nostrils flaring. The dogs, egged on by Krisela, danced about the horses' legs, nipping at their ankles. In the midst of it all, Gregor and Jayson were locked in combat.

Kemp pressed down on Gregor's throat. Gregor, pinned beneath him on the ground, clawed at Kemp's hand and fought to free himself. I caught Krisela's eye and signaled for her to control the dogs. One sharp whistle and the dogs left off worrying the horses and trotted to her side. With the dogs in check, she grabbed the nearest set of reins and set about calming the horses.

Now that the animals were out of the way, I stepped up to the two men who still grappled in the dust. Images of Jayson kidnapping the two sisters, dragging them through the forest, and tying them up played through my mind. I let the rage that had been seething inside me for hours take over. Grabbing Jayson by the back of his shirt, I yanked him off of Gregor and flung him aside.

Jayson fumbled to his feet, his face a mask of anger and surprise. He focused on me, let out a roar, and barreled toward me. *Four seconds*, my combat-ready mind informed me. I blinked. *Three seconds*. I dropped my weight and adjust my stance to prepare for impact. *Two seconds.* My right hand curled into a fist. *One.* A split second before he reached me, I took a step forward and my fist collided with his jaw in a loud crunch.

Kemp's hand flew to his face before he reeled back and collapsed in a heap, his long cloak swirling before it settled around him.

I stood over him, half hoping he would rally so that I might have another go. But he didn't stir. I turned to Gregor and offered him a hand. "Are you all right?"

He allowed himself to be pulled to his feet. "Not as young as I used to be, I'm afraid."

"You should have let me take the front while you took the rear."

"And pass on the honor of landing the first punch?" The glint in his eye caused the corner of my mouth to twitch.

The comment that it seemed he had plenty of fight left in him never left my lips. My attention was claimed by the scuffle of several sets of feet on the dirt floor. I turned to see three men at the front entrance.

"It's about time!" Kemp hollered.

"Wha—" A white-hot burning in my calf cut the question short. I spun to see Jayson crouched behind me with a red-slicked blade in one hand and a triumphant look on his face.

"Leave them to me," Gregor growled, heading in the opposite direction. "You see to Kemp."

"Get 'em, boys!" Krisela called out a second later, her voice louder than I had ever heard it. Growls, sharp barks, and the sounds of paws breaking into a run answered her.

I ignored the ensuing screams and yelps. My vision closed in on the knife in Kemp's hand. The rage coursing through me guided my actions. *Distraction.* With the uninjured leg, I kicked dust into Kemp's eyes. Before he could reel back to clear his sight, I stepped forward and grasped his wrist in one hand and twisted. I met his eyes, watching as the triumph faded. The blade clattered to the ground. Jayson dropped to the floor as I released him.

I grabbed the knife from the floor and thrust it through my belt, all the while pinning Jayson in place with a glare. "If you know what's good for you, you'll stay down."

The noise behind me had tapered off. I hazarded a glance at the entrance. The dogs had two men backed into a corner. The hounds' low growls could be heard. The third man lay on the floor, Gregor's foot pressed to his throat.

I pitched my voice loud enough for all of them to hear. "You will have no further contact with any member of Lord Bromhurst's family, is that clear?"

The two men in the corner agreed readily; the man under Gregor's heel groaned. Jayson rubbed at his wrist and treated me to stony silence, his eyes reproachful.

I nudged him with a boot—though it was probably more of a kick—and inquired a second time. "Do you understand?"

He grumbled assent.

"Good." I peered down my nose at the piece of scum who considered himself worthy of a place at Lady Ariela Spencer's side. "If I ever find that you have done otherwise," I glared at the other three men as well, "you will have me to reckon with." Now that it was no longer silenced by fury and action, the pain in my calf began throbbing dully. It would have to wait. "Gregor?"

"Yes?"

"Can you see about delivering these men to the authorities?" I pulled the ropes from my pocket and tossed them to him.

"It would be my pleasure."

"I'll help!" Krisela called out. She took a length of rope from Gregor and knelt to secure Jayson's hands. A whimper sounded as Krisela tightened the knots around Kemp's wrists.

"Oh dear, does that hurt?" she asked, giving the rope another yank.

"I'll leave you to it." I nodded, watching Gregor expertly hog-tie the man on the ground. I grabbed the reins of two of the horses and headed out the same way I had entered. The pain running up from my calf grew from the movement, and the back exit seemed further away than before. I gritted my teeth against the ache and moved slowly.

"Is it done?" Braden asked, popping his head in the door right before I reached it.

"Everything according to plan. More or less." I kept my face as passive as possible and handed him a set of reins.

"According to plan? Who planned on three men barreling in the front entrance just when you had everything under control? I had a difficult time keeping these two from rushing in when they heard the scuffle. What was that all about, anyway?"

"Later." I sent him a warning look. "How are the ladies?" If Ari didn't know what had happened, it was best to keep it quiet. Who knew how she might react? I scanned the area for her. Seated on a nearby log, she rubbed at her wrists where the ropes had been. For a moment, I wished she were the type of woman who would race toward her rescuer and cover him in kisses.

"They're shaken by the experience, but otherwise unharmed, I believe."

I shuffled toward her, careful not to cringe at the throbbing caused by the motion. I searched her face for some clue as to how she was feeling. "Did he hurt you?"

She stood, brushing off her skirts and avoiding my eye. "Not particularly." Her voice was tight.

For someone who had tried to push past Braden to come to my aid, she acted very aloof. The feeling of relief that had begun to settle over me after disposing of Kemp was disrupted by a tightening in my chest. The watchful eyes of the group warned me to wait for a more private moment to question her. I couldn't wait. "Then what is it?"

"If you don't mind, we'll head back," Braden interrupted. Larela and Brisella were already mounted on a horse. Braden stood at its head. "It appears that you have some things to discuss." He gave me a meaningful look.

Brisella turned around in the saddle. "Thank you, Jonas."

I nodded and watched the trio disappear around the corner of the building. I let out a breath. The wound in my calf hurt more than ever and fatigue had begun to take effect. I longed to be in bed with someone to fuss over me, but that wasn't to be. Imagining Ari decked out in a maid's uniform hand-feeding me soup didn't help matters either. I looked inside the warehouse, hoping Gregor and Krisela needed my help. Two of the men were already lashed to the pommel of one horse while another was slung over the saddle. With a grunt, Gregor hefted the last hog-tied captive onto a mount and nodded at Krisela to lead the horses out of the building. He patted the nearest dog on the rump and the two hounds followed the entourage outside.

"Well done, Jonas," he called out, "We'll take these four in and leave the last mount tied at the front for you."

I nodded grimly.

Gingerly, I made my way to the log where Ari had sat a moment before and lowered myself onto it. "Why do I have the feeling that Braden knows more about whatever it is that's bothering you than I do?"

Ari wouldn't meet my eye. "Braden is amazingly perceptive."

It wasn't a term I would regularly use to describe Braden, though lately he had shown surprising ingenuity and, yes, perceptiveness. With the pain in my calf gnawing at me, my patience began to wear thin. "It's been a very long day, Ari. If you have something to say, come out with it."

Her fingers fidgeted, twisting together and releasing, and then fluttering over her skirts to brush the wrinkles from them.

"Please." To top off everything—the exertions of the day, the years of standing at her side and longing for more, the wound burning in my calf—I was nothing more than a farm boy at heart. Courtly phrases meant to flatter and tease the truth out of women were beyond me.

"You'll think me foolish."

The words surprised me. In the midst of all the chaos and drama of the day, Ari had not blubbered or begged but had maintained her composure. If I knew anything about her, she had tried to fight back as well. "That's impossible."

She gazed at me through lowered lashes, probably gauging if I was in earnest.

I wanted to wrap her up in my arms and put an end to these silly ideas. But that would require standing, something my leg wouldn't tolerate at the moment. I patted the spot beside me on the log, inviting her to sit. When she settled beside me, I said, "I could never think of you as foolish."

"I've acted like a complete idiot." She buried her face in her hands, the flow of tears I would have expected earlier now wet her cheeks.

I leaned closer and put an arm around her, wincing as the movement caused pain to shoot up my leg. I bit my lip to hold it in and cradled her as she wept.

After a moment, I said, "Since I met you, you've always been the most beautiful and brilliant woman I know."

She sniffled and leaned back.

"Not an ounce of stupidity," I added.

She wiped at her eyes with a corner of her cloak. "Running off to dance the night away with villagers?"

I conceded with a nod. "Maybe not your most brilliant of plans, but perfectly executed."

Her eyes narrowed.

"No," I said, repositioning myself because my leg had begun to stiffen. "It's the truth. I'm too exhausted to mince words just now."

Her brows drew into a straight line and her eyes narrowed. "Jonas, what have you done to yourself?"

I shrugged a shoulder and looked away. Her glare bore into me.

"Show me."

I hesitated. Ari's thundercloud expression grew darker with each second. "Kemp had a knife," I explained, gesturing toward the injury. "It's nothing serious."

Her hand flew to her mouth when she saw the red staining the leg of my trousers. She dropped to a crouch in front of me to examine the wound.

"Really, it's nothing," I said, as she lifted the pant leg to assess the damage.

Her anger faded to pity, pulling the corners of her mouth down. Wordlessly, she tore a piece of her underskirt to clean the cut.

"It's not that bad. I've gotten worse from the bull at home." True as it was, it didn't ease the concern from her brow. "Someday I'll show you the scar."

Carefully she wrapped a length of fabric around the gash and tied it in place.

"Does it hurt?"

"No," I lied, my voice higher than I would have liked.

With great care, she lowered the trouser leg over the bandage. Her sigh was almost imperceptible as she settled once again at my side. "I'm so sorry, Jonas. This is all my fault."

"I don't think I'd go that far," I tried to tease. "It wasn't your knife."

She leaned her head on my shoulder. "You know very well that I could have prevented all of this." Her fingers curled around mine. "I allowed my sisters to carry on in this ridiculous fashion month after month, just to spite my father. Then, I let myself be duped by that idiot Jayson. How could I ever have thought it was you who wrote that note?"

Though everything she said was true, I refused to hold it against her. "How could you have known?"

She squeezed my fingers and made no other reply.

"Besides, I'm the one who turned my back on the man. I should have guessed he would be armed."

"Shhhh," she pressed a hand to my mouth. "Allow

me to say it, Jonas."

I held perfectly still, breathing in her soft scent, reveling in her nearness, and hoping she would say the words I wanted to hear most.

A tiny grin played at her lips. "I acted like a lovesick schoolgirl running away like that."

My lips curved up at her admission.

"I really did think I was running to you. It's fortunate that Bree wouldn't let me go alone. Who knows what Jayson might have done if I had."

The words were muffled by her hand still pressed over my mouth. "You didn't try to fight back?" It had been the one thought running through my mind the entire time. Ari wasn't the type to allow anyone to take advantage of her. She removed her hand from my lips.

"I was worried for Bree's safety. I might have gotten away, but I couldn't guarantee she wouldn't be hurt. When we did try something in the woods, he threatened Bree with the knife."

I remembered the torn cloak in the forest. "We found her cloak."

Her brow furrowed.

"He didn't hurt her?"

"No. He lunged at her to frighten her and sliced her cloak by accident. At that point, I thought it best that we bide our time and try to reason with him later." Absently, she traced circles over the back of my hand. "We were formulating a plan for escape when the doors of the warehouse crashed open and Gregor, Kris, and all the animals piled in." The hint of laughter flavored her tone. "Was it your plan?"

I imagined the mad scene, orchestrated to distract Jayson's attention while we whisked his captives out the back. I shrugged.

"Of course it was."

I shrugged again. "You knew I would come."

She wrinkled her nose. "Jonas Selkirk? Everybody's hero? I did expect you to make an appearance."

The urge to drop a kiss on that wrinkled up nose hit me. "Back to what you said before," I mused. "Something about acting like a lovesick schoolgirl?"

She snuggled into the spot between my shoulder and my neck. "Did I really say that?"

"I've just been through a hellish day and may now be mortally wounded because of you," I scoffed. "The least you can do is admit it."

"I never would have told you to turn your back on Jayson Kemp. Weasel or not, he's devious."

My mouth hung open.

"You look like a codfish, Jonas," she said primly. With a finger, she pushed my chin up until my teeth clicked shut. "And you said it was just a scratch, didn't you? Or were you just trying to be manly?" She pointed down at my leg.

I didn't remember saying that, but a haze of exhaustion and pain clouded my mind. "Now you're just trying to distract me."

"From what?" she asked, her light eyes wide with innocence.

"Fine." I disentangled my fingers from hers and with an effort, rose to my feet to stand in front of her. I paid no heed to the pain shooting up from my calf and focused all my attention on Ari. Tucking my hands behind me, I began, "If you behaved like a lovesick schoolgirl, my behavior has only been slightly less ridiculous. My first impulse was to run after you and pummel into submission whoever had taken you."

The tiny grin returned to her face. "My hero."

"If the others hadn't been levelheaded, I don't know what I would have done. As it was, when Braden tried to charge pell-mell into the warehouse, I wanted to beat him to it."

The grin widened.

"But Lady Ariela Spencer, have no doubt that my actions were motivated by nothing other than pure, unadulterated love." I cocked my head to the side and conceded, "And maybe jealousy."

She laughed up at me as she had done a thousand times over the years. That toss of the head and her burble of laughter never failed to make my pulse race. They also never failed to make me feel like a complete idiot.

I wasn't finished. "Today, I have risked everything to come to your aid. If, by the end of day, I'm not dismissed from the household outright, the punishment I will suffer at Gregor's hand will indeed be severe." Even acting on my best intentions as I had done today wouldn't save me from whatever punishment he deemed just.

"However," I kept my face serious and tried to ignore the mirth playing about Ariela's mouth, "I would do it all again if your love is my reward."

She rose to her feet, her eyes sparkling, and took my hands in hers. "Oh, Jonas," she said, running her thumbs over the back of my hands, "even if you hadn't come for me today, I would still love you."

"And what would your father say to that?" I meant it as a joke, but her face fell, I could almost see the thoughts flashing through her mind. A man of influence could do much to part us, especially someone as determined as Lord Bromhurst.

"Well, there's no point in concealing it now," she stated. "He'll learn everything soon enough. If he'd been paying attention, he'd have realized that my heart was spoken for long ago."

The words warmed me, but I wouldn't let them deter me from what I had to say next. I focused on her hands, small and delicate, nestled in mine. "There's still time to change your mind. You needn't live the life of a pauper's wife. You can remain here, as Lady Ariela."

The offer was met with silence. I struggled to keep my nerves in check. She deserved the life of a noblewoman. Some part of me wanted her to go on living it, whether or not I was a part of it.

"Jonas," she said, waiting until I looked into her face. I noted the straight line of lips and the soberness in her eyes. "My decision has been made."

Larela

The manor loomed before us. I slowed the horse and felt Ariela's arms tighten around my waist. She peered around me at the building. "Should we use the other entrance?" The suggestion sounded ridiculous. Under no circumstances would Lord Bromhurst's daughters ever use the service entrance.

"It's no use, they've already seen us."

A flurry of movement started at the front entrance. Footmen carrying word of our arrival to His Lordship, no doubt, and ladies' maids preparing to fuss over Ariela.

"No matter what happens," she said as she leaned against my back, "it doesn't change anything."

My chest expanded. I had won the woman of my dreams. My moment of triumph lasted mere seconds, however, before the buzz of servants scurrying about by the entrance interrupted it. Two figures detached themselves from the group. The shorter of the two jogged toward us while the other strode purposefully behind him. The first, Braden, reached us in a matter of minutes.

"What took you so long?" he asked in a rush of breath.

I raised my eyebrows. Gregor drew up behind him.

"Well, um," Braden muttered, averting his eyes. "I meant to say that Lord Bromhurst is awaiting the return of his eldest daughter. Anxiously."

"That's one way to put it," Gregor growled out. "You'd better hurry along. And it's probably best if you don't arrive with her ladyship behind you in the saddle."

I felt my face flush.

"Oh please," Gregor added with a groan. "Of all the things that have come to light, this is the least surprising." He motioned toward the two of us.

"You knew?" Ari asked. The same question had been floating through my mind. I remembered his guess that the warehouse was the site of the ladies' midnight outings and his lack of surprise over Braden's familiar treatment of Larela.

"Of course." He looked me up and down. "And don't think for a moment that I ever would have let this good-for-nothing gardener out of my sight if I thought he would do you any harm."

If my eyebrows had raised any further, they would have joined my hairline.

"I know everything that goes on in these grounds. Did you think it was just coincidence that no one found the two of you together over the years?" Gregor narrowed his eyes. "Surely you can't be that much of a simpleton, Jonas."

Apparently I was. "Braden caught us once," I countered.

"Slippery as an eel that one." He shook his head in disdain.

"Not to be a killjoy, but shouldn't we be going?" Braden interrupted.

I glanced back at Ari. "Perhaps it's better if we—"

"Face the music?" she finished primly, allowing Braden to help her down. "We may as well."

I slid down after her, keeping the reins in my hand, and wincing as my wounded leg hit the ground with a zing of pain. I leaned against the horse for a second until the throbbing dropped back to a dull ache. I squeezed the reins tightly, gritted my teeth, and followed Braden and Ari with the horse clopping behind us.

"How much does my father know?" Ari asked.

"Only what he's been told," Gregor replied. "That you were escaping to town each night to dance with the locals and that one of them kidnapped you and Lady Brisella. He had his suspicions, but it seems that he knew nothing with any certainty until today."

"He may have guessed more." Ari tossed me a glance, then refocused on Gregor. "How angry is he?"

Gregor's grim expression settled into place.

"Well, if I had to say . . ." Braden said. "Then—"

At this point a female figure hurried out of the front

doors and down the steps. The servants parted for the Master's youngest daughter.

"What is taking so long?" Larela demanded as soon as she was close enough. "Father is ready to burst!"

Ari cast me a repentant look. She took her sister's hand and patted it, trying to calm her. "Everything will be fine. You'll see, Lari."

Larela towed Ari by the arm toward the manor. "You say that now, but you haven't seen him yet."

We reached the group of servants clustered around the front steps. I passed the horse off to a nearby stable boy and climbed the stairs a pace behind the others. The throbbing in my calf intensified with each step.

The massive doors loomed over me. My experience with wealth, luxury, and entitlement didn't extend beyond serving those who possessed them. My own parents' home boasted a weathered wood door with peeling paint and a dull knob scuffed from years of use. It was nothing compared to this.

The footman stationed beside the entrance cleared his throat. I glanced around at the group standing nearby. All eyes were fixed on me, gawking up at the great doors while the rest of the party had entered. No time left to stall. I drew a breath and passed through the open doors and into the entry hall. With twin staircases winding upward on either side, a vast marble floor, and a large chandelier hanging above, it was even more impressive than the front entrance. Suddenly, I felt exactly like the country bumpkin who had arrived over a decade before, knock-kneed, inexperienced, and overwhelmed by everything with which he came into contact.

An even larger company, including servant and gentry alike, filled the hall. Few of them marked my arrival. In that moment, I wanted nothing more than to fade into the line of waiting servants as I had been trained to do. Anonymity meant safety. But it also meant forgetting everything that had happened between Ari and me in the past two days.

Ariela had already moved toward the center of the hall, her back straight and her head held high. Only the tightness in her shoulders hinted at her nerves. I couldn't abandon her. I stepped up beside Braden, only a couple of steps behind Ari.

Everyone fell quiet as Lord Bromhurst strode toward his daughter, his footsteps ringing on the marble floor. His brows and mouth were pulled down in an expression as heavy as his gait. Ari's shoulders dropped half an inch. The urge to step between Bromhurst and his eldest daughter hit me. I held my ground.

Lord Bromhurst reached Ari and stopped. My fists clenched and I pressed them against my sides. The glare on his face grew darker as he looked his daughter up and down. My teeth ground together and my jaw tightened. In a movement so quick I could never have intervened, Lord Bromhurst stepped forward and buried his eldest daughter in an embrace. If Ari's twinge was anything to go by, it was bone crushing. A public display of affection with an undercurrent of malice seemed fitting given His Lordship's recent treatment of his daughters.

"Relax." Braden's hand pressed into my sternum. Only then did I realize that I too had stepped forward. I took a step back, shook out my hands, and released the breath I'd been holding. A gnawing at the pit of my stomach warned me to keep a close eye on my master.

Lord Bromhurst eased up after a moment and held Ari at arm's length to look her over again. "He didn't hurt you, did he?" The show of fatherly concern hung on him like a garment he hadn't worn for ages.

From the expression on Ari's face, she too found it surprising. "I'm quite all right, Father," she said.

"No lasting damage?" He checked her over for bruises or signs of abuse. Nothing more was visible than the faint rope marks on her wrists.

"Nothing too terrible," Ari replied.

"I warned you about this." His tone switched from concern to reprimand in the blink of an eye. "You'd be better off married and in your own home rather than gallivanting across the countryside with village boys." He took a deep breath, preparing to launch into a full tirade.

Someone cleared his throat. With a cursory glance behind him, Bromhurst released his breath and looked slightly abashed. Lord Gillingham and his son, both looking ill at ease, stood behind him.

"Quite right," Bromhurst muttered, taking his daughter's hand and turning her to face us. He proceeded in a louder voice, "We are grateful for the stalwart staff who acted quickly and courageously." His gaze shifted to someone behind me. "Gregor, I believe we have you to thank for my daughters' safe return."

Gregor never sought praise, but only a fool would deny it when it came his way. He cleared his throat. "With all due respect, My Lord, Jonas Selkirk planned the rescue mission." He motioned toward me.

I felt my face blanch as the focus shifted to me. Beside me, Braden's face flushed an angry red.

"And young Braden," Gregor added, almost as an afterthought.

From the superiority on the Master's face, I could tell he considered me below his notice. "I owe you a debt of gratitude." He bowed his head a fraction of an inch.

Without missing a beat, Braden stepped up beside me. "Our pleasure, My Lord." He swept into a low bow. When I didn't respond, he jabbed me in the ribs with an elbow. I offered a stiff bow and something approximating a smile of acceptance.

"Your intervention comes at the perfect moment," Lord Bromhurst stated with a broad grin. He motioned behind him. "Come forward, Gillingham. These are the men you have to thank for the return of your betrothed."

"Father," Ari said, tugging on his arm.

"Hush, child," he said, dismissing her. The flash of anger across his face invited no further argument.

Irritation bubbled inside me; I pushed it down and kept my temper in check. Lord Gillingham paused before me with his hand extended and friendliness spread over his face. I hesitated, feeling that I'd rather knock him flat. Instead, I too extended my hand. Clasping mine in both of his, Lord Gillingham pumped it up and down in a hearty handshake.

"We are most grateful. Mr. Selkirk, wasn't it?"

I nodded, remembering the precarious position in which I found myself. I couldn't afford to be thrown out yet. Not without my wages and a solid reference from Gregor in hand. Besides, the man before me was respectable and kind. Grinding his smiling face into the marble floor simply for being the man Ariela's father intended her to marry was pointless.

"Thank you, Mr. Selkirk." His face split in a wide grin.

He stepped up to Braden next. "And you must be Braden. Much obliged."

Braden nodded, completely at ease in the nobleman's presence. "I am glad to be of service, Your Lordship."

"Now, Gillingham," Lord Bromhurst said, glowing with pride as he pulled Ari forward, "take her hands in yours."

Looking too eager for my taste, Lord Gillingham took both of Ari's hands in his. Everyone about me murmured with pleasure. The muscles in my jaw tightened. I clenched my teeth against words that wanted to push their way out.

"Everything is as it should be," Lord Bromhurst declared, clapping his hands together. "I see no reason to delay the happy event." He caught the eye of a nearby footman and called out, "Send for the vicar! The wedding will be held tonight!"

The room around me erupted into applause. My heart hardened into a cold lump. Even with my teeth clenched together, somehow one word still made it out. "No."

The elation on Lord Bromhurst's face was replaced by surprise. "Pardon me. What was that?"

My voice cut across the sounds of mirth. "Lady Ariela will not marry this man. Tonight or ever."

The company fell silent, the warmth evaporating from the room. Lord Bromhurst took long strides toward me, stopping when our faces were inches apart. In a harsh whisper, he said, "Do not mistake my gratitude for indulgence, boy. I am well aware of your attachment to my daughter. I care little what feelings you harbor for her. If you make one move to disrupt these proceedings, your dismissal will only be the beginning of the misery I will rain down upon you."

I squared my shoulders and spoke aloud. "With all due respect, My Lord, Ariela does not love him."

The look on Lord Bromhurst's face was murderous. "What business is it of yours?" he demanded. "And what right do you have to call my daughter by her Christian name?"

Gregor stepped forward, placing himself at my side. "My Lord, might I remind you that Jonas risked everything to save your daughter's life. He has already proven that he has her best interests at heart."

I had never expected anything of the sort from

Gregor. Disapproval, punishment, a stern talking to, yes. Defending me before the Master? Absolutely not.

"This is none of your concern, Gregor," Bromhurst spat out. "However, be certain that I will remember where your loyalties lie as well as the ill behavior of those you have trained."

Gregor's shoulders bowed under the weight of His Lordship's displeasure. The sight rankled like a burr caught in my trouser leg.

"He is not to blame." I pulled myself up to my full height, a couple of inches taller than the Master, and met his eye. "Gregor is one of your most loyal servants. He ensures that everyone in his stewardship shows the utmost respect for the household and its rules."

"The same rules that you have broken today?" Lord Bromhurst trained his glare back on me. "Then, if this isn't a lapse in your education, am I to understand that this is nothing more than bad breeding?"

The intentional slight on my family would normally have been enough to call me out, but I couldn't afford the luxury. For Ari, I must keep my temper in check. I spoke for all to hear, "You are to understand that I love your daughter and I desire to marry her."

The company at large drew back, but their eyes remained riveted on us. Lord Bromhurst stared at me, stunned into silence.

"And I would have him as my husband." Ari placed her hand on his arm. He shook it off. A muscle in my cheek started to switch.

"This is ludicrous!" Bromhurst poured the full

weight of his rage on his eldest daughter. "He's a gardener, Ariela. I will not allow you to waste yourself on such a man!"

The fire I knew well ignited in Ari's eyes. "I wouldn't care if he were a traveling peddler with a cart full of tawdry wares. He's the man I love."

The eyes of the entire group bore into me, taking in my plain clothing and sizing up the man who dared to claim a woman so far above him.

The Earl's hand flew before I could react; the resounding slap pierced the stillness. Ari clapped a hand to her cheek.

"You are still my daughter!" he spit out the words. "I forbid you to marry this man!"

I pushed Ari behind me and faced her father, rage burning in my veins. "You will never touch her again."

"She is my daughter! I will do as I see fit!" he bellowed. "If I say that she will wed Gillingham, then that is precisely what she will do!"

I spoke calmly "Lady Ariela has already proven adept at dodging your commands, My Lord. If you demand that she marry Lord Gillingham, I promise you that nothing will stop her from escaping before the ceremony is performed."

He stared at me, his mouth agape. No one ever spoke to him in this manner, much less a servant.

"And I will help her," I added.

The silence in the room lengthened out as Lord Bromhurst looked from Ari to me. "Ridiculous!" he bellowed, the sound causing the chandelier overhead to tinkle. "You'd never run away with this . . ." he faltered for a moment, "this commoner." Coming from his mouth, the word sounded like the worst sort of profanity.

Ariela stepped around me to stand at my side.

"Might I remind you that you are betrothed," he said through gritted teeth, "to the Earl of Gillingham."

"Not that you asked my opinion on the matter," Ari said, "but Lord Gillingham is twice my age. I will not throw my life away on a man I do not love." My words coming out of Ari's mouth took me by surprise.

"Gillingham is twice the man *he* will ever be!" her father bellowed, motioning at me. "What does he have to offer?"

"His heart in exchange for mine," Ari answered quietly.

"Love?" Lord Bromhurst snarled. "You will find it poor currency, my child. Where will you live with your gardener? You know full well I will not house you here. What use will you be to him without your title and money?"

"My family will see to our needs," I answered.

"Common country folk?" Distaste curled his mouth into a sneer.

"Farmers actually," Ari replied with a lift of her chin. "Who, unlike those who believe themselves to be superior in rank and breeding, care for their own."

"You," he said, jerking his chin at me. "You would give up your position in a respectable household for this?"

I didn't reply. I kept my gaze firmly locked with his.

"You claim to love my daughter, but you would allow her, a noblewoman, to live in squalor?"

"If it means she no longer has to live under your rule or suffer abuse at your hand, then so be it."

"I could have you arrested for meddling with my daughter," Lord Bromhurst threatened.

"I would have a word to say about that," Lord Gillingham said, his round face stern. "That man rescued your daughter, Bromhurst. If Lady Ariela prefers him to any other, as is obviously the case, then I, for one, will not stand in the way. I withdraw my petition for your daughter's hand in marriage."

Lord Bromhurst swallowed this down, his throat working as if the pill were indeed a bitter one.

"Please, Father." Brisella appeared at his side. "They've done nothing wrong. Just let them be."

He looked at Brisella, the anger in his face fading. "Is no one to take my part?" One glance around the room was enough to reveal that each of his daughters, as well as Lord Gillingham and his heir, stood their ground.

He refocused on Ariela. "Get out of my sight," he said coldly. "If this is to be, I'll have nothing more to do with you."

Ari's hand trembled in mine.

I wrapped an arm around her slim shoulders and steered her toward the door. Her dowry, social status, and family connections would be forever lost. For me, ten years of employment were wasted. No type of recompense or reference would be forthcoming. The future stretched before us, a steep uphill path, bleak and unchanging. We passed the group of nobles, our steps dull on the marble floor. My leg throbbed with our slow progress toward the exit. I did my best not to limp.

Ari, sniffling slightly, offered me a grim smile. I swiped at the one tear that trickled down her cheek. How could I be miserable with such a woman beside me?

"No!" The word came out shrill and insistent. I glanced over my shoulder. The group eyed Larela warily. "Father, you can't allow this to happen!"

"They have chosen their path. What would you have me do?"

"Send them with some money, give them a home in the village! Anything!" The frantic tone reminded me of a younger Larela on the verge of a tantrum. "If you let them leave like this, you'll never see Ariela again."

Lord Bromhurst's eyes were shuttered and his lips pressed into a line. "I will do nothing."

She turned to Braden. "Then you must do something. Now."

"What would you have me do, My Lady?"

An expression not unlike the one her father wore appeared on her face.

Braden emitted a sound like a chuckle, but devoid of mirth. He glanced between Larela and Ariela and me. Then he turned back to Larela and executed an elegant bow, "Only for you, My Lady." He cleared his throat and addressed Lord Bromhurst. "Your Lordship, I must intervene on behalf of your eldest daughter and my friend, Jonas Selkirk."

"Tread carefully, young man," Lord Bromhurst said. "Throwing in your lot with theirs will earn you the same punishment."

"Generally, that is the way of things," Braden agreed. "But we both know how these situations can be glossed over by men of your influence. Society need never know that you listened to the counsel of an undergardener or allowed your daughter to marry a farmer."

Anger flickered in the older man's eyes. "I believe I have made myself clear," he said, "My daughter has chosen a life of poverty. I can do nothing for her."

"Surely you don't wish to send your eldest daughter off to an uncertain future," Braden stated. "Imagine," he said slowly, his eyes glinting like a card sharp savoring the moment before he dropped his trump onto the pile, "if your family had behaved in such a manner when *you* chose to wed a woman far below your station."

I watched Ari's reaction. Every feature, from slack mouth to wide eyes, displayed surprise.

"Imagine if your father had disowned you when he learned that you had fallen in love with a *commoner?*" Braden's pointed use of the word wasn't lost on Lord Bromhurst.

Bromhurst looked green, though his eyes and tight lips held more than a hint of anger.

"Years ago, men of influence acted on your behalf. Because they accepted your betrothed into good society, few people learned of your wife's common beginnings."

Lord Bromhurst swallowed. "How do you . . . how do you know about that?"

I wondered that as well. It was obvious that no one else in the room, including the late Lady Bromhurst's own daughters, knew her history.

"That's unimportant. The issue at hand is whether or not you would punish your daughter for following in your footsteps?"

Braden's query hit its mark. Lord Bromhurst looked at Ariela for the first time since he had dismissed her. His eyes were more deeply shadowed and the lines around his mouth were more severely cut into his cheeks. His face held the same regret that painted Ari's features.

"Let me guess," Braden continued. "The moment your eyes fell on Katherine McCleary, her beauty and sweetness overcame you. It took little time to realize that she possessed more gentility than any of the women of your acquaintance. It didn't matter that she had no money or prospects. You fell in love with her just the same."

Weariness showed in every feature. Lord Bromhurst made no move to deny Braden's words.

"What did your family do when they discovered your attachment?" Ariela asked quietly.

He cast his gaze to the floor, his shoulders bowed.

"Don't you see?" Ari said. "All I want is a portion of the same generosity you and mother were shown."

Lord Bromhurst closed his eyes. When he spoke, fatigue rather than anger flavored his tone. "It changes nothing."

Ari released a frustrated sigh.

If the man were so heartless that he would cast aside his own child for doing the same thing he had done, we'd be better off on our own. Once more, I steered Ariela away from the group and toward the wide doors.

"If that is your final word on the subject, My Lord," Braden said with utmost diplomacy, "there is little point in arguing the matter."

Relief washed over me at Braden's words. Much as I hated to admit it, he had become like a brother. It would be unbearable if he were punished for championing my cause.

"However, before you bid farewell to Lady Ariela forever," Braden continued, "you might like to know everything about the man she has chosen to marry."

I couldn't help but wonder at this new tactic.

Lord Bromhurst scoffed, a touch of his anger returning. "You try my patience, boy. It's time you left me in peace."

"Jonas is descended from a long line of respectable farm folk," Braden stated, paying no heed to Bromhurst's last comment. "From Stone or thereabouts, if I remember correctly."

We reached the wide doors leading outside, but Braden's words held me in place a second longer. I pressed a hand to the doorframe, my mind whirling. I looked him over, trying to guess his motives. His confident stance betrayed no concern whatsoever.

"You've wasted enough of my time. Now, if you don't mind—" Lord Bromhurst made as if to brush past Braden.

"I haven't finished, My Lord," Braden said, with such authority that it held even Lord Bromhurst in place. "The Selkirk family, though little more than commoners, are closely tied to the Dukedom to the north."

I exchanged a glance with Ari. She too had turned to watch the scene unfold. The same confusion I felt sketched across her features.

"You'd have me believe that the Duke of Trentwich and his family have dealings with farmers?" Lord Bromhurst asked in disbelief, clearly wondering why he hadn't thrown Braden out the second he had spoken up. "Rubbish."

"Ordinarily, I would agree," Braden said, nodding. "However, I assure you that Jonas Selkirk is a close confidant to the duke's son and heir."

Rubbish is right, I thought. There was no way Lord Bromhurst would buy the lie no matter how skillfully Braden peddled it.

"Ludicrous," Lord Bromhurst declared. "The duke's son hasn't been seen in some time." He peered down his nose at Braden. "Besides, no nobleman would allow himself intimacies with someone so far beneath him."

With his shoulders squared and his chin lifted,

Braden didn't look as if he were ready to relent. "In this case," he said, as his hand dipped under the collar of his rough shirt. He pulled forth some type of chain, "it's nothing but the truth." Whatever hung on the end of the chain glittered under Lord Bromhurst's nose.

As one, the company leaned in for a glimpse of whatever it was that hung from Braden's fingers. Mutterings passed through the group. Only Lord Bromhurst's words were loud enough to make out. "Your Lordship."

Braden

Astonishment and incredulity filled my mind, each vying for a place. Facts clicked together like puzzle pieces and pushed both emotions aside. Braden's courtly manner—which charmed every female in the household—and his resourcefulness in dangerous situations were both out of character with the persona he portrayed at work. He'd always been more like a young boy on an adventure. Even in the coarse dress of an undergardener, everything about his bearing declared the truth. Braden had been born for something far grander than tending kitchen gardens.

Beside me, Ari's mouth formed a silent *oh*.

"The title hardly seems necessary, Lord Bromhurst," Braden said. "I hadn't meant to make myself known so soon. My sole motive in doing so is to ensure the happiness of my friends."

"Of course, Your Lordship," Braden's former Master babbled. "No one would doubt your motives."

"How did you find yourself in service to Lord Bromhurst, I'd like to know," grumbled the one person in the circle who wasn't overawed by Braden's newfound status.

Braden chuckled. "That's a story for another time, Gregor. But, I can tell you that anyone with enough money and resources can disappear from the public eye and reinvent himself as an undergardener."

Gregor shook his head in disapproval. "And now?"

"I suppose I'll have to return to my father," he said matter-of-factly. "Once all of this is settled, of course." He motioned for Ari and me to approach with a decidedly courtly wave of the hand.

"Is that how you knew about my mother?" Ari asked, her hand still tucked in mine as we stopped before Braden.

"Yes. There is little that gets past my father," Braden replied, a note of pride flavoring his tone. "Many years ago, he heard of your father's predicament and was kind enough to aid in hushing it up." A cockeyed grin spread across his face. "My father has always had a soft spot for romance."

"Well, Bromhurst, what do you have to say for yourself?" Lord Gillingham interrupted. "Disowning your daughter seems a poor way to honor those who aided you in the past. Mr. Selkirk is clearly a decent fellow and a far better son than you deserve."

Bromhurst, who had refused to be swayed by anything thus far, wilted under the censure of his peer.

"If you would be so indulgent," Braden said,

bowing to Gillingham, "I believe I have the perfect solution." He turned back to Lord Bromhurst. His demeanor was serious, but his eyes twinkled. "The estate is yours, isn't it Bromhurst? None of that nasty entailment business, is there?"

"No . . ." Lord Bromhurst drew the word out. "The estate is mine to do with as I please."

"Since you have no male heir, it stands to reason that you would settle it upon one of your daughters. Correct?"

Ari, whose mind worked much faster than mine, squeezed my hand tightly.

Lord Bromhurst narrowed his eyes. "What do you propose?"

"On one hand, I could petition the crown to bestow land and a title on Jonas. It might take some time, but it could be brought about in the end. Of course, I would receive all the credit for bringing a man of such caliber to court . . ."

"And on the other hand?"

"You could make Ariela your heir. Permanently and irrevocably. Of course the title will return to the male line as soon as Lady Ariela bears a son." He nodded at Brisella, who stood alongside Lord Richard Comstock, Gillingham's heir. "If I don't miss my mark, your second eldest will be mistress of her own estate soon enough."

Lord Gillingham spoke up. "Just so. All that has happened here today has only strengthened my resolve. I will personally see to it that Lady Brisella is well provided for, Your Lordship."

"Very well." Braden trained his eagle eye on his former master. "What do you have to say, Bromhurst?"

An air of suspense hung in the room, enveloping nobility and servants alike as they waited for Lord Bromhurst's edict. My heartbeat thrummed in my ears and sweat gathered on my brow.

"The alternative being," Braden stated, "that you follow through in disowning your daughter. Of course, I would be honor bound to send word to my father. He in turn would undoubtedly have a private conversation with His Royal Highness, the King, about your conduct. Given your past, who knows what action the King might deem appropriate?"

The color again drained from Lord Bromhurst's cheeks. As plain as day, I could see the thoughts flicking through his mind. He knew the dangers of displeasing royalty. At the very least, his actions could result in public censure, the equivalent of a slap on the wrist. However, if the King deemed Lord Bromhurst's conduct as contemptible, it might lead to the seizure of his lands.

"My boy," Lord Bromhurst said to me, the smile stretching his lips and showing far too many teeth. "Welcome to the family."

The company about us broke into awkward applause. Under the cover of noise, Lord Bromhurst leaned in to whisper harshly, "Don't believe for one second that I approve, but as there is nothing else to be done, for this moment, you have won."

Everyone around us murmured in pleasure at what looked like a show of acceptance. Ari and I exchanged a glance. One thing was sure, we would not only have to be on our best behavior, but we'd have to make certain her sisters toed the line as well.

Lord Bromhurst clapped a heavy hand on my shoulder. I tried not to wince. He spoke loudly. "After all, you did save my eldest daughters from injury and ruin, Jonas. It's only fitting that you be rewarded accordingly." The eyes behind the wide smile were flat and cold. "You have my blessing."

When Bromhurst released me, Braden caught my eye and raised both eyebrows. A corner of his mouth twitched. Boxing a nobleman's ears wouldn't be tolerated, I reminded myself, especially not now that I knew he was a nobleman.

Some sort of gracious acceptance would be expected, even though Lord Bromhurst had insulted my family and publicly disowned his daughter less than fifteen minutes earlier. I took a deep breath and reminded myself of what weighed in the balance: the happiness of my would-be bride and her eleven sisters.

"Thank you, Your Lordship." I executed the type of bow Braden had modeled. "It will be my greatest honor to unite my family with yours."

"Now that everything's decided," Braden announced. "Bromhurst, Gillingham," he nodded at both men in turn. "Shall we retire to the dining hall? Surely the staff can be induced to pull some type of dinner together." He flashed a grin at a nearby kitchen maid. "Everyone is undoubtedly famished."

Several female servants curtsied in his direction, all the more smitten upon learning of his elevated station. They hurried off in the direction of the kitchens and dining hall along with half of the staff. The rest returned to their posts while the four noblemen, eleven ladies, and everyone else made their way to the dining area.

Ariela and I stood in the middle of the marble entryway and watched the others file off. I wrapped an arm around her shoulders, inhaled her fragrance, and breathed out a sigh of relief. "The Duke of Trentwich . . . it's unbelievable. How will we ever repay him?"

"I believe he considers the debt paid in full." She nodded toward the front of the departing group, where Larela hovered as close to Braden as convention allowed. "He'll make her a duchess. Father certainly won't disapprove of that connection."

"The upper class has all the luck." I shook my head. "I take it I'm to be the disreputable son-in-law, then?"

"Disreputable . . ." The word rolled off her tongue while a tiny smile played about her mouth. "I find that rather attractive. It's sort of dangerous, isn't it?"

I held out my arms to better display my plain shirt and trousers, now smudged with dirt, sweat, and blood from the brawl with Jayson. "I suppose I might pass as rakish."

"Hmmm," she mused, "That's almost as good as disreputable." She snuggled against my chest.

I wrapped my arms around her, enjoying the fact

that I could do so in the light of day. With witnesses.

"Who could have believed Jonas—the unassuming gardener—capable of concocting a rescue plan, beating a man in hand-to-hand combat, and saving damsels in distress?"

"There's so much you've yet to learn about me," I said, looking down my nose at her and trying to sound superior.

She gazed up at me through her lashes. "There will plenty of time for that."

My heart caught in my throat. They would not be the stolen moments of yesterday, but rather years upon years with Ariela at my side. I rested my chin on her head and thought of the days to come. There would be plenty of time to learn everything there was to know about one another. There would be time to create a family together.

"It's unbelievable," I repeated, thinking of the curly headed lads and straight haired lasses that would come into the world. They would be ours. "With men like Lord Gillingham and a duke's runaway heir on hand, why would you choose me?"

Ari arched back, running a speculative eye over me. "Well," she said slowly, "you're a good deal younger than the last man I found myself betrothed to, so that's a point in your favor. And of course the money is a consideration."

I felt one corner of my mouth turn down. "I'll bring little enough of that to the union."

"Then marry me for my money," Ari said. "Doesn't

Lady Ariela Selkirk have a lovely ring to it?"

I nuzzled her ear and murmured against her neck, "It does indeed."

"Hmmm . . ." Ari purred as I tilted her chin up and dropped kisses along her jaw. "If my father tries to wriggle out of it, I know a certain Lord Braden MacDonald who might be inclined to convince him."

I nodded, then shook my head. "I think he's done enough."

Ari let out a small chuckle. My arms settled more tightly around her. The feeling of rightness pushed aside the memory of countless yesterdays without her in my arms.

"So, you're going to marry me for my money?" she teased, plying her lips to my earlobe.

My brain melted into jelly at her touch. Only one word made it out. The same stubborn word that always worked its way out. "No."

She left off nibbling my earlobe. My scrambled mind thanked her for allowing me to think for a moment. Other parts of my anatomy were less pleased.

"No?" she repeated. "My father's money, then?" Her arms wrapped around me more snuggly and her lips hovered a tantalizing inch from mine.

"No."

Her breath mingled with mine as she brushed her lips over my mouth. Agony. Ecstasy. My thoughts settled on the nearby staircase leading to secluded places in the mansion that were abandoned at this time of day. One sweep of the arms and I'd be carrying her up them and then—

There was something more important. Something that nagged at the back of my mind. What was it again?

"No one tells a lady no," Ari said, her voice low and her eyes dreamy as she placed a tiny kiss beside my mouth. "And certainly not twice in a row."

The hazy thought surfaced like a leaf floating on a stream, spinning and as it reached the top. "No," I said at last, "I will not marry you for your money. Or your father's money."

She kissed the other corner of my mouth and rested her cheek against mine to whisper, "Three times? Unforgivable, Jonas."

I denied the urge to flip her over my shoulder and make for the staircase. Gingerly, I took her face in my hands and looked into her eyes. Light brown, filled with affection. The rest of her might age, but those eyes would remain the same. "Lady Ariela, I will marry you for one reason only."

"And what is that?" Her slim eyebrows lifted in question.

I took a breath, searching for the words. After all that had depended on selecting the perfect words for her father, much more depended on this. "I can't live without you."

A broad smile pressed lines into her cheeks. "I know just what you mean," she said, pressing her smile to mine and muffling every other thought in a blissful haze.

Acknowledgements

Writing a novel is never a solo performance. Well, okay, I *did* write *Midnight Sisters* on my own, but if it weren't for all the awesome individuals who kept me on track, you wouldn't be reading it today. First and foremost, thanks goes to my family. They are the type of people who may not see each other every day, but they show up for the big stuff, like holidays, broken collar bones, and book launches. I thank the heavens every day that I have them. Incidentally, they're the inspiration for the Selkirks.

Next up are the amazing women in my life. The mamas, besties, sisters-in-law, cousins, aunties, and more who served as inspiration both for my life and this novel. Thank you, ladies. This sister of five brothers couldn't have figured out the difference between manicures and pedicures or womanhood and girlhood without you.

A special thank you to the talented Cindy Iverson

for designing the cover and managing the finer details of my technical needs. I love you forever. And not just because I have to. You're a genius!

And entering the big bad indie publishing world would've been a lot scarier without the reassuring words of Misty Pulsipher and Jo Ann Schneider. Thanks for blazing the path, girls! And for keeping me calm during a process that could've been a lot harder.

As for Meg Zerkle, the best editor a girl could ask for, I'm glad to have you on my side, sweetie. Thank you for helping me make my book so much better than I could have on my own. And thanks for talking me out of a tree at least ten times this year. I'll always love you for that, and for so many other things.

Last of all, I want to thank you, my dear readers. Thank you for loving fairytales as much as I do and for believing in magic. Never underestimate the power of love, family, or a good pair of schmancy shoes.

Discussion Questions

1. Historically, nobles were esteemed based on their titles and land holdings. Their interactions with the serving class were formal and limited. Like Jonas and Ariela, romance did surpass class distinctions from time to time. Is it reasonable to expect such individuals to bow to social convention and put an end their relationships? Does this stigma exist in modern society today?

2. Jonas Selkirk would do anything for love. He turns his back on everything he values—his position and chance for betterment—to run to the aid of his ladylove. Would you consider his actions foolhardy or gallant? Discuss what you would or would not do for a loved one in a difficult situation.

3. Each night Lord Bromhurst's daughters escape their boring lives to dance the night away. They must go to great lengths to keep the truth from their father

and maintain their freedoms. If you could escape to a magical land of your choice, would you pay the price to do so?

4. Braden trades his position and status as a nobleman to live and work as a servant. How can obligations become so overwhelming that a person considers dropping out of the limelight completely? In what circumstances would you consider doing something similar?

5. The twelve sisters differ in temperament, talents and looks, but they are bound by ties of friendship and sisterly love. Who do you relate with the most? Why?

6. The Earl of Bromhurst holds to traditional roles for men and women. He only allows his daughters to engage in ladylike pursuits while he does as he pleases. What gender stereotypes are present in modern society? How can this inspire individuals to work for change?

Author's Note

While *Beauty and the Beast* is my favorite fairytale (hence the birth of *Becoming Beauty*) *The Twelve Dancing Princesses* is second on the list. A dozen sisters dance their shoes to pieces every night while soldiers, princes, and men from all walks of life struggle to unravel the mystery and win the fair maiden. Then there's the magic at the heart of the tale: a land of gold and silver forests, a glittering lake, and a bejeweled palace.

Hmmm . . . Let me think about that for a minute. Dancing the night away in a froufrou gown and bedazzled dancing slippers with the prince of your choice? Where do I sign up for that gig?

Transforming *The Twelve Dancing Princesses* into a story without magic was relatively easy once I caught the thread of family woven throughout. As a girl who was raised with wolves (a.k.a. five brothers), imagining the trouble twelve sisters could get into was intoxicating. I had no idea how fun it would be to gift that many girls with distinct personalities and random quirks. Or how horrifying it would be to have them boss me to within an inch of my life once I did so. Fully immersing myself in a world of women in their teens and twenties was like rubbing elbows with the sisters I never had. I'll be forever grateful to the sisters of my heart who inspired the noblewomen in *Midnight Sisters* and filled that precious role in my life.

In case you're wondering, there were a couple of retellings that set my feet on the path toward *Midnight Sisters*. The first is the beautifully illustrated children's book, *The Twelve Dancing Princesses*, retold by Marianna Mayer and illustrated by K.Y. Craft. I fell in love with this book the moment I set eyes on it. The second is the *Twelve Dancing Princesses Series* created by Jessica Day George. In that incomparable way of hers, George breathes life and magic into the flat fairytale princess characters with whom we grew up.

About the Author

Sarah E. Boucher is a lover of fairy stories, romance, anything BBC and Marvel, and really, really cute shoes. On weekdays she wears respectable shoes and serves as Miss Boucher, the Queen of Kindergarten. On school holidays she writes stories about romance and adventure. And wears impractical super cute shoes.

Sarah is a graduate of Brigham Young University. She lives and works in northern Utah. *Midnight Sisters* is her second novel. Connect with Sarah online on Facebook, Twitter, Instagram, Goodreads, Amazon, or by visiting her website at saraheboucher.com

Made in the USA
Columbia, SC
15 July 2024

38433801R00159